William Shakespeare's Henry VIII: A Retelling in Prose

David Bruce

Published by David Bruce, 2022.

WILLIAM SHAKESPEARE'S HENRY VIII: A RETELLING IN PROSE

First edition. July 26, 2022.

Copyright © 2022 David Bruce.

ISBN: 979-8201544546

Written by David Bruce.

Table of Contents

Educate Yourself
Read Like A Wolf Eats
Be Excellent to Each Other
Books Then, Books Now, Books Forever

***

In this retelling, as in all my retellings, I have tried to make the work of literature accessible to modern readers who may lack the knowledge about mythology, religion, and history that the literary work's contemporary audience had.

Do you know a language other than English? If you do, I give you permission to translate this book, copyright your translation, publish or self-publish it, and keep all the royalties for yourself. (Do give me credit, of course, for the original retelling.)

I would like to see my retellings of classic literature used in schools, so I give permission to the country of Finland (and all other countries) to give copies of this book to all students forever. I also give permission to the state of Texas (and all other states) to give copies of this book to all students forever. I also give permission to all teachers to give copies of this book to all students forever.

Teachers need not actually teach my retellings. Teachers are welcome to give students copies of my eBooks as background material. For example, if they are teaching Homer's *Iliad* and *Odyssey*, teachers are welcome to give students copies of my *Virgil's* Aeneid: *A Retelling in Prose* and tell students, "Here's another ancient epic you may want to read in your spare time."

OMID ABBASI

On 14 May 2013, fire broke out in an apartment building in Tehran, the capital of Iran. Omid Abbasi and other Iranian firefighters arrived to fight the fire. Learning that a seven-year-old girl was trapped inside, Mr. Abbasi rushed into the building and found the girl. To keep her alive, he gave her his oxygen mask. He rescued the girl, but he suffered brain death due to lack of oxygen, although doctors in a hospital emergency room tried to save his life. After he died, his family donated his organs to three patients who needed transplants. His mother said, "He was kind and loved saving people." The little girl attended Mr. Abbasi's funeral and said, "He saved my life, and I am really thankful." Reddit user D3VO_Lution commented, "I will never cease to be amazed by the sheer selflessness of some people in this world."

CAST OF CHARACTERS

Male Characters

King Henry VIII.

Cardinal Thomas Wolsey. He is Archbishop of York and also Lord Chancellor. The Lord Chancellor is custodian of the Great Seal.

Cardinal Campeius.

Capucius, Ambassador from the Holy Roman Emperor Charles V.

Thomas Cranmer, later Archbishop of Canterbury.

Duke of Norfolk.

Duke of Buckingham.

Duke of Suffolk. His name is Charles Brandon, and he married Mary Tudor, King Henry VIII's sister.

Earl of Surrey, Buckingham's Son-in-Law.

Lord Chamberlain.

Lord Chancellor.

Gardiner, Secretary to the King; later Bishop of Winchester.

Bishop of Lincoln.

Bishop of Ely.

Bishop of Rochester.

Bishop of Saint Asaph.

Bishop of Canterbury.

Lord Sands.

Sir Henry Guildford.

Sir Thomas Lovell.

Sir Anthony Denny.

Sir Nicholas Vaux.

Secretaries to Wolsey.

Cromwell, Servant to Wolsey; later Secretary to the Privy Council.

Griffith, Gentleman-usher to Queen Catherine.

Three Gentlemen.

Doctor Butts, Physician to the King.

Garter King of Arms. The Garter King of Arms is the King of England's heraldic advisor; he is an expert on ceremonials and heraldry.

Former Surveyor to the Duke of Buckingham. He oversaw the Duke of Buckingham's estates.

Brandon.

A Sergeant-at-Arms.

Doorkeeper of the Council Chamber.

Porter, and his Assistant.

Page to Gardiner.

A Crier.

Female Characters

Queen Catherine, First Wife to King Henry, afterwards divorced and becomes Princess Dowager.

Anne Boleyn, her Maid of Honor, afterwards Henry VIII's Second Wife and Queen.

Old Lady, Friend to Anne Boleyn.

Patience, Woman Servant to Queen Catherine.

Minor Characters

Several Lords and Ladies in the Dumb Shows.

Women attending upon the Queen.

Scribes, Officers, Guards, and other Attendants.

Spirits.

Scene:

London; Westminster; Kimbolton.

***Nota Bene*:**

Anne Boleyn is Anne Bullen in Shakespeare's play, and Catherine is Katherine in Shakespeare's play. I have used the spellings that are most often used in our time.

Catherine is Catherine of Aragon; she married King Henry VIII in 1509, and they were divorced on 23 May 1533.

Archbishop of Canterbury Thomas Cranmer pronounced the marriage of King Henry VIII and Anne Boleyn valid on 18 May 1533. The marriage had taken place on 25 January 1533, but was kept secret until Anne became noticeably pregnant.

Anne Boleyn was crowned Queen of England on 1 June 1533, and she gave birth to the future Queen Elizabeth I on 7 September 1533.

William Shakespeare is thought to have co-written this play with John Fletcher.

PROLOGUE

The Prologue speaks directly to you, the readers:

"If I remember correctly, the last time I appeared before you, it was in a comedy, but I come no more to make you laugh. We the characters now present things that bear a weighty and a serious aspect. They are solemn, lofty, and moving, full of stateliness and woe, such noble scenes as draw the eye with tears to flow.

"Those who can feel pity, may, if they think it good to do, let a tear fall here while reading this work of art. The theme of our work of art will deserve such pity.

"Such as give their money out of hope they may believe what they read, may find truth here, too.

"Those who come to read about only a spectacle or two will approve of this work of art, if they will be still and willing to pay attention. I'll venture to say that they may agree that their small amount of money was well spent for the few short hours it takes to read this work of art.

"Only they who come to read a merry and bawdy work of art and to imagine a noise of swords against shields or to imagine seeing a fellow in a jester's long motley coat trimmed with yellow will be disappointed.

"Gentle readers, you should know that our work of art shows the truth we choose to focus on. To rank it as of equal worth to such a show as is filled with fools and fights, besides forfeiting the labor of the brain and characters that created this work of art and forfeiting the goal that we have of revealing only truth, will leave us no understanding friends and audience. Such readers who rank it like that misunderstand what we are attempting to do.

"Therefore, for goodness' sake, and as you are known as the best and happiest readers of the town — you are reading this in London, aren't you? If you aren't, pretend that you are — be serious as you read this, as we want you to be. Imagine that you see the very persons of our noble story as if they were living. Imagine that you see them great and high on the Wheel of Fortune, and followed by the general throng and sweat of a thousand friends, and then in a moment, see how quickly the Wheel of Fortune turns and this mightiness meets misery.

"And, if you can be merry then, I'll say that a man may weep upon his wedding day."

5

CHAPTER 1
— 1.1 —

In an antechamber — a small room leading to a large room — in the palace in London, the Duke of Norfolk met the Duke of Buckingham and Lord Abergavenny. Lord Abergavenny was one of the Duke of Buckingham's sons-in-law.

The Duke of Buckingham said to the Duke of Norfolk, "Good morning; we have met at a good time. How have you been since we saw each other last in France?"

"I thank your grace," the Duke of Norfolk said. "I am healthy, and ever since I left France I continue to be an enthusiastic admirer of what I saw there."

"An untimely bout of fever made me a prisoner in my chamber when those Suns of glory, those two lights of men — King Henry VIII of England and King Francis I of France — met in the valley of Andren," the Duke of Buckingham said.

They were talking about a summit held between the two Kings from 7 to 24 June 1520 in the Field of the Cloth of Gold.

The Duke of Norfolk said, "It was held between the English-held town of Guynes and the French-held town of Ardres. I was present and saw the two Kings salute on horseback. I also saw, when they dismounted, how they clung in their embracement, as if they grew together. And if they had grown together and formed one compounded King, what four enthroned Kings could have equaled such a compounded one?"

The Duke of Buckingham said, "The entire time I was a prisoner of illness in my chamber."

The Duke of Norfolk said, "Then you lost the view of Earthly glory. Men might say that until this time of the meeting of the two Kings pomp was single, but now pomp is married to one above itself. With the meeting of the two Kings, pomp moved to a higher level, as if it had married into a higher social class.

"Each following day became the next day's master, until the last day made all former wonders its own. Each day was more splendid than the previous day.

"One day the French, all glittering, all in gold, like heathen gods made of precious metals, outshone and out-glittered the English. But the next day, the English made Britain appear to be wealthy India. Every English man who stood looked like a gold mine. Their dwarfish pages were similar to cherubim, all in gold. The ladies of rank, too, not used to toil, almost sweat to bear the proud and splendid attire upon them, so that their labor made their faces red as if they were wearing blush.

"This masque was cried incomparable, but the ensuing night made it in comparison seem to be a fool and beggar.

"The two Kings, equal in luster, were now best, now worst, according to which one was present. Whoever was in the public eye was always the one receiving praise, and when both Kings were present, people said they saw only one King because the two Kings were equal in splendor. No discerning viewer dared to wag his tongue in censure and rate one King higher than the other.

"When these Suns — for that is what people called the two Kings — had their heralds challenge the noble spirits to arms, the two Suns performed beyond what was thought possible, so that stories that were formerly thought to be fabulous fabrications were now seen to be possible enough, and so the old stories got credit and even the improbable stories about the hero Bevis, the protagonist of the verse romance *Bevis of Hampton* who battled giants, dragons, and other mythological creatures, were believed."

"Oh, you go too far," the Duke of Buckingham said.

"As a noble of high rank who loves and seeks honesty in matters of honor, I say that the relation of everything that happened would lose some life even when told by a good raconteur. The actions spoke for themselves far better than even a good storyteller could.

"All was royal. Nothing rebelled against its management. Everything was arranged so that each sight was clearly visible, and each official performed his duty perfectly and with distinction."

The Duke of Buckingham asked, "Who guided — I mean, who set the body and the limbs of this great entertainment together, do you guess?"

"One, certainly, who does not lead one to expect him to be a part of such a business," the Duke of Norfolk said.

"Please tell me whom you mean, my lord," the Duke of Buckingham said.

"All this was arranged by the good discretion of the right reverend Cardinal Wolsey of York."

"May the Devil — not God! — make him prosper!" the Duke of Buckingham said. "No man's pie is freed from his ambitious finger — he has a finger in every pie. What business had he with these fierce vanities? I wonder that such a keech can with his very bulk take up the rays of the beneficial Sun and keep them from the Earth."

A keech is the fat of a slaughtered animal, fat that has been rolled up into a ball. Cardinal Wolsey was both fat and the son of a butcher.

The Duke of Buckingham knew, of course, that Cardinal Wolsey was a powerful man who had the ear of King Henry VIII. He felt that Cardinal Wolsey was preventing King Henry VIII from doing good things for England. Cardinal Wolsey was using his fat bulk to keep the Sun's — Henry VIII's — beneficial rays from reaching England.

The Duke of Norfolk said, "Surely, sir, there's in him stuff and qualities that cause him to do such things. For, since he is the son of a butcher, he is not propped up by a noble ancestry, whose grace shows successors their way to success, nor is he acclaimed for high feats done on behalf of the crown. Neither is he allied with eminent assistants; he has no important connections. Instead, like a spider, out of his self-made web, he let us know that the force of his own merit makes for him a passageway to success — his merit is a gift that Heaven bestows on him, and his merit buys for him a place next to the King. He lacks a good family, notable deeds of service, and good connections, but nevertheless he has other qualities that Heaven gave him that enable him to make for himself a position next to King Henry VIII."

Lord Abergavenny said, "I cannot tell what Heaven has given Cardinal Wolsey — let some graver eye than mine pierce into that, but I can see his pride peep through each part of him. Where did he get that pride? If he didn't get it from Hell, then the Devil is niggardly and keeps all the pride or has already given it all away. If Cardinal Wolsey didn't get his pride from Hell, then he begins a new Hell in himself."

A proud person regards himself as the center of the universe. Out of pride, Lucifer rebelled against God. Lucifer was thrown out of Heaven and fell to Earth, where he hit with such impact that he reached the center of the Earth. His fall created the nine circles of Hell that Dante writes about in his *Inferno*.

Dante believed that the Earth was the center of the universe, and since Lucifer is at the center of the Earth, Lucifer is at the center of the universe. Pride created Hell, and if Cardinal Wolsey did not get his pride from the previously existing Hell, then he is creating a new Hell with his pride.

The Duke of Buckingham said, "Why the Devil, upon this expedition to France, did Cardinal Wolsey take upon him, without the participation and knowledge of the King, to appoint who should attend on him?

"Cardinal Wolsey makes up the list of all the gentry who attend on the King. For the most part those on the list are those whom Cardinal Wolsey means to extract as much money and give as little honor as he can in return. Without consulting the honorable Board of Council, aka the Privy Council, he sends his letter to the nobles and they accompany the King and pay great expenses."

The Duke of Buckingham objected to the great expense of such an expedition to France. He believed that the whole Board of Council, and not just Cardinal Wolsey, should decide which nobles would accompany King Henry VIII on such a foreign expedition.

Lord Abergavenny said, "I know of at least three kinsmen of mine who have by this action of Cardinal Wolsey so sickened their estates that they will never again be as wealthy as they were previously."

The Duke of Buckingham said, "Oh, many have broken their backs with laying manors on them for this great journey."

Nobles would sell manors in order to buy fabulously expensive clothing for such an expedition.

The Duke of Buckingham continued, "What good did this expensive vanity accomplish? The two Kings met and conferred, but the result of their conference was very poor, and it impoverished the children of the nobles forced to accompany our King."

"I grieve when I say that the peace treaty made between the French and us was not worth the cost that it took to make it," the Duke of Norfolk said.

"After the peace between England and France was made, a hideous storm followed, and every man became an inspired prophet. Without previously consulting each other, they all made the same prophecy — they said that this tempest, destroying the garment of this peace, foretold the sudden breach of the treaty."

"And the prophecy turned out to be true," the Duke of Norfolk said, "for France has broken the peace treaty and has confiscated the goods of our merchants at Bordeaux."

Lord Abergavenny asked, "Is that the reason Cardinal Wolsey has silenced the French ambassador and has placed him under house arrest?"

"Yes, it is," the Duke of Norfolk replied.

Lord Abergavenny said sarcastically, "What a 'good' peace treaty, and purchased at such a highly wasteful rate!"

The Duke of Buckingham said, "Our reverend Cardinal Wolsey has managed all this business. He is the one responsible."

The Duke of Norfolk said, "May it please your grace, the government is aware of the private quarrel between you and the Cardinal. I advise you — and take it from a heart that wishes towards you honor and much safety — that you take into account both Cardinal Wolsey's malice and his power. He is a formidable enemy. Consider further that he does not lack the power and agents to do to you whatever his great hatred of you wants to do. You know his nature; you know that he's revengeful. And I know that his sword has a sharp edge. His sword is long and it reaches far, and where it will not extend, there he shoots an arrow. Take my advice to heart — you'll find it wholesome."

He then said, "Look, that rock that I advise you to shun and avoid is coming. Unless you steer clear of that rock, you will shipwreck."

Cardinal Wolsey, who was also Lord Chancellor, walked into the anteroom. A bag containing the Great Seal, an emblem of the Lord Chancellor, was carried before him. Some members of the guard and two secretaries holding papers accompanied him.

Cardinal Wolsey and the Duke of Buckingham stared at each other with hatred. They were far enough apart that they could not hear what the other said.

Cardinal Wolsey said to the first secretary, "Where's the deposition of the Duke of Buckingham's surveyor?"

The Duke of Buckingham's surveyor was actually his former surveyor. He had been recently fired as the overseer of the Duke of Buckingham's estates.

The first secretary replied, "Here it is, if it please you."

"Is he here in person and ready to give evidence?" Cardinal Wolsey asked.

"Yes, if it please your grace," the first secretary replied.

"Well, we shall then know more, and Buckingham shall not look at me with such a haughty look."

Cardinal Wolsey and his train of attendants exited.

Referring to Cardinal Wolsey's parentage, the Lord of Buckingham said, "This butcher's cur — mean dog — is venom-mouthed, and I don't have the power to muzzle him; therefore, it is best that I not wake him from his slumber. Let sleeping dogs lie."

He added, "A beggar's book learning is regarded more highly than a noble's blood."

"What, are you angry?" the Duke of Norfolk said. "Ask God for temperance; that's the only remedy that your disease requires."

The Duke of Buckingham said, "I read in his looks that he intends business against me, and his eye reviled me as if I were an object of contempt to him. At this instant, he is wounding me with some trick. He has gone to the King. I'll follow and outstare the Cardinal."

"Stay here, my lord," the Duke of Norfolk said, "and reason with your anger. Question what you are thinking about doing. To climb a steep hill requires a slow pace at first because hasty climbers have sudden falls. Anger is like a high-spirited horse, which being allowed its way, its high spirits soon tire it.

"Not a man in England can advise me like you do. Be to yourself as you would be to your friend. Take for yourself the advice you would give to your friend."

"I'll go to the King," the Duke of Buckingham said, "and from a mouth of honor quite cry down this Ipswich fellow's insolence, or else I will proclaim there's no distinction of rank or quality among people and a butcher's son is as good as a Duke."

Ipswich was the provincial town from which Cardinal Wolsey came.

"Be advised and take thought," the Duke of Norfolk said. "Don't heat a furnace for your foe so hot that it singes yourself."

He was alluding to the story of Shadrach, Meshach, and Abednego in Chapter 3 of the Book of Daniel. They were thrown into a fiery furnace, but God protected them; however, the men who threw them into the fiery furnace died from the fire. While Shadrach, Meshach, and Abednego were in the fiery furnace, a fourth figure who resembled the Son of God was seen with them.

Daniel 3:19-22 states this:

19 Then was Nebuchadnezzar full of rage, and the form of his visage was changed against Shadrach, Meshach, and Abednego: therefore he charged and commanded that they should heat the furnace at once seven times more than it was wont to be heated.

20 And he charged the most valiant men of war that were in his army, to bind Shadrach, Meshach, and Abednego, and to cast them into the hot fiery furnace.

21 So these men were bound in their coats, their hosen, and their cloaks, with their other garments, and cast into the midst of the hot fiery furnace.

22 Therefore, because the king's commandment was strait, that the furnace should be exceeding hot, the flame of the fire slew those men that brought forth Shadrach, Meshach and Abednego. (1599 Geneva Bible)

The Duke of Norfolk continued, "We may outrun, by violent swiftness, that which we run at, and lose by over-running.

"Don't you know that the fire that heats the liquid and makes it rise until it run over the pot, although it seems to augment the liquid, actually wastes it?

"Be advised: I say again that there exists no English soul better to direct your course of action than yourself — if with the sap of reason you would quench, or at least lessen, the fire of passion."

The Duke of Buckingham said, "Sir, I am thankful to you; and I'll go along with your advice to me, but this proud-to-the-top fellow, about whom I say not from the flow of anger but from sincere motives, from reliable information, and from evidence and proofs as clear as streams in July when we see each grain of gravel, that I know him to be corrupt and treasonous."

Streams get muddy when dirt is washed into them; in the Duke of Buckingham's experience, streams in July tend to be clear.

The Duke of Norfolk said, "Don't say the word 'treasonous.'"

The Duke of Buckingham said, "To the King I'll say it, and I'll make my accusation as strong as a shore made of rock. Listen to me. Cardinal Wolsey is a holy fox, or wolf, or both — for he is equally as ravenous as he is subtle, and as prone to mischief as he is able to perform it; his mind and place infecting one another, yes, reciprocally."

He was referring to two sayings about animals: as subtle — sly — as a fox, and as ravenous as a wolf.

He continued, "Cardinal Wolsey, only to show his pomp as well in France as here at home, persuaded the King our master to accept this recent costly treaty and the meeting of the two Kings that has swallowed so much treasure, and the treaty is like a glass that broke as it was being rinsed."

In this culture, drinking glasses were expensive.

The Duke of Norfolk said, "Truly, the peace treaty broke as easily as a drinking glass."

"Please, let me continue to speak, sir," the Duke of Buckingham said. "This cunning Cardinal Wolsey drew up the terms of the peace treaty as he himself pleased, and they were ratified as he cried 'Thus let it be,' to as much purpose as giving a crutch to a dead man, but our Count-Cardinal — our upstart Cardinal who tries to act like a Count — has done this, and it is well, for worthy Wolsey, who cannot err, did it. I am being sarcastic, of course.

"Now this follows — which, as I take it, is a kind of puppy to the old dam, treason — Holy Roman Emperor Charles V, under the pretense to see Queen Catherine, his aunt — for it was indeed his stratagem, but he really came to whisper to Cardinal Wolsey — came here and visited.

"Holy Roman Emperor Charles V's fears were that the meeting between the King of England and the King of France might, through their amity, breed him some misfortune, for from this peace league peeped harms that menaced him. He privately dealt with our Cardinal Wolsey, and I know well — I am sure about it — that Holy Roman Emperor Charles V paid before Cardinal Wolsey promised to do as the Emperor wished, and so the Emperor's suit was granted before it was asked.

"In short, Holy Roman Emperor Charles V got what he wanted from Cardinal Wolsey because before asking for what he wanted, he had already paved the way with gold. Holy Roman Emperor Charles V asked that Cardinal Wolsey would break the aforesaid peace treaty with France to alter the King's planned course of peaceful action.

"Let the King know, as soon he shall learn from me, that thus Cardinal Wolsey buys and sells King Henry VIII's honor as he pleases, and for his own advantage. Cardinal Wolsey accepts bribes to do the bidding of people other than his King."

The Duke of Norfolk said, "I am sorry to hear this of him, and I could wish that he were somewhat misjudged in it."

"No, he has not been misjudged," the Duke of Buckingham said. "Not a syllable of what I have said about him is incorrect. My report about him describes him exactly as he shall be proved to be."

Brandon entered the antechamber, along with a Sergeant-at-Arms and two or three members of the Guard.

Brandon said to the Sergeant-at-Arms, "Your duty, Sergeant; execute it."

The Sergeant-at-Arms said, using all the titles of the Duke of Buckingham, "Sir, my lord the Duke of Buckingham, and Earl of Hereford, Stafford, and Northampton, I arrest you for high treason, in the name of our most sovereign King."

The Duke of Buckingham said to the Duke of Norfolk, "Look, my lord, the net has fallen upon me! I shall perish because of a plot and trickery."

Brandon said, "I am sorry to see your liberty taken from you, and I am sorry to look on this present business, but it is his highness' pleasure that you shall be taken to the Tower of London."

The Duke of Buckingham said, "It won't help me at all to plead my innocence, for a dye has been placed on me that makes my whitest part black. May the will of Heaven be done in this and all things!

"Brandon, I will do as you say.

"Oh, my Lord Abergavenny, fare you well!"

Brandon said, "No, he must bear you company in the Tower of London."

Brandon said to Lord Abergavenny, "The King wishes you to be taken to the Tower of London until you know what he decides to further do."

Lord Abergavenny replied, "As the Duke of Buckingham said, may the will of Heaven be done, and may I obey the King's pleasure!"

Brandon said, "Here is a warrant from the King to arrest Lord Montacute and to arrest the bodies of the Duke's confessor, who is named John de la Car, and one Gilbert Peck, his Chancellor —"

"I see," the Duke of Buckingham said. "These are the parts that make up the plot. No more will be arrested, I hope."

Brandon replied, "A monk of the Chartreux."

"Oh, Nicholas Hopkins?" the Duke of Buckingham asked.

"Yes, him," Brandon replied.

"My surveyor is false," the Duke of Buckingham said. "He lies and commits perjury. The over-great Cardinal Wolsey has shown him gold and bribed him to tell lies about me. My life is spanned already. The extent of my life has been measured, and its string is about to be cut.

"I am the shadow of poor Buckingham, whose figure even this instant cloud puts on, by darkening my clear Sun.

"I, poor Buckingham, am now only a shadow of what I was. This instant cloud — this immediate accusation — darkens my blameless life and takes my character and even my body away from me."

He then said to the Duke of Norfolk, "My lord, farewell."

King Henry VIII, leaning on Cardinal Wolsey's shoulder, walked into the Council Chamber of the palace in London. Sir Thomas Lovell and some other nobles accompanied them.

Henry VIII sat on a throne on a dais. Cardinal Wolsey sat on a lower level on the King's right side.

The King then said to Cardinal Wolsey, "My life itself and its most vital essence — the heart — thank you for this great care you have taken of me. I stood in the line of fire of a fully loaded conspiracy, and I give thanks to you for suppressing it."

He then ordered, "Let be called before us that gentleman of Buckingham's. In person I'll hear him confirm his confessions, and he shall again relate point by point the treasons of his master."

Outside the room, someone shouted, "Make way for the Queen!"

Queen Catherine entered the Council Chamber, accompanied by the Duke of Norfolk and the Duke of Suffolk. She went to the King and kneeled.

King Henry VIII rose from his chair of state.

Using the royal plural, Queen Catherine said, "No, we must continue to kneel. I am a petitioner to you."

"Arise, and take a seat by us," King Henry VIII said.

He raised her up from her kneeling position, kissed her, and then moved her beside him.

He then said, "You don't need to ask me to grant half of whatever you want because you have half of our power. The other half, before you ask me for it, is granted to you. Tell me what you want, and it is yours."

Queen Catherine replied, "I thank your majesty. The point of my petition is that you would love yourself, and in that love not leave unconsidered your honor or the dignity of your office. What I want is what is best for you, and it will not require that you lose your honor or the dignity of your position."

"My lady, continue speaking," King Henry VIII said.

"I have been solicited, not by a few, and by those of true and loyal disposition toward you, to inform you that your subjects have a great grievance and are in great distress. Tax levies have been sent down among them that have flawed the heart of all their loyalty to you."

She said to Cardinal Wolsey, "Although, my good Lord Cardinal, they vent reproaches most bitterly against you as the putter on of these extortionate taxes, yet the King our master — whose honor may Heaven shield from being soiled! — even he does not escape being the target of impolite and rude language, yes, such language as breaks the sides of loyalty, and almost appears in the midst of loud rebellion."

"Not 'almost appears,'" the Duke of Norfolk said. "It does appear, for upon receiving these notices of taxation, all the clothiers who make woolen clothing, no longer able to maintain their many employees, have laid off the spinsters who spin the wool, the carders who comb the wool, the fullers who beat the wool to clean and thicken it, and the weavers. These unemployed people, unable otherwise to make a living and compelled by hunger and lack of other means to maintain life, in desperation are daring the event to the teeth — they are accepting the dire consequences that follow from rebellion. They are all in uproar, and danger is their servant!"

"Taxation!" King Henry VIII said. "Where? And what kind of taxation? My Lord Cardinal, you who are blamed for it alike with us, do you know about this taxation?"

Cardinal Wolsey replied, "If it pleases you, sir, I know only of a single part — one person's share — in anything that pertains to the state. I am only the most conspicuous among those who march along with me. In other words, I am only one man among other men, although I am the most conspicuous among those men."

Queen Catherine disagreed: "No, my lord. You know no more than others, but you bring to pass things that are known by everyone who marches along with you — by others in your council. You originate things such as taxes that are not wholesome to those who don't want them and yet are forced to pay them.

"These exorbitant taxes, about which my sovereign wants to have information, are very pestilent to those who bear them. In bearing these exorbitant taxes, the back is sacrificed to the load — people are sacrificed because they are considered less valuable than the taxes they pay.

"People say that the exorbitant taxes were devised by you, Cardinal. If that isn't true, then you suffer too hard an exclamation of outrage against you."

"Still talking about exorbitant taxes?" King Henry VIII said. "What is the nature of these taxes? What kind of taxation is this? Let me know that."

Queen Catherine said, "I am much too bold in testing your patience, but I am emboldened under your promised pardon."

King Henry VIII had already promised to give her whatever she wanted.

Queen Catherine continued, "The subjects' grief comes through tax commissions, which compel from each a sixth of his wealth, to be given up without delay; and the excuse given for this tax levy is your wars in France.

"This exorbitant taxation makes mouths bold. Tongues spit their duties out, and cold hearts freeze their allegiance within them. Your subjects' curses now live where their prayers did, and it's come to pass that your subjects' tractable, compliant obedience has become a slave to each incensed will.

"I wish that your highness would give that matter quick consideration, for there is no more important business than this."

"By my life, this is against our pleasure," King Henry VIII said.

Cardinal Wolsey said, "As for me, I have gone no further in this than by a single vote. That taxation was not imposed by me but by the learned approval of the judges of the council.

"If I am traduced and slandered by ignorant tongues, which know neither my capabilities nor me as a person and which yet want to be the chronicles of my actions, let me say that it is only the fate of a high position and the rough thicket that virtue must go through.

"We must not refrain from doing our necessary actions just because we are afraid to encounter malicious censurers — malicious censurers who always, as ravenous fishes do, follow a newly outfitted ship, but benefit no further than vainly longing."

Sharks can follow a ship in hopes that it will sink and they can dine on sailors, but a newly outfitted ship is in good repair and unlikely to sink. Or sharks can follow a newly outfitted ship that has just set out on a journey in hopes of eating tossed-overboard food garbage, but a ship that has just set out on a journey will probably have no food garbage to throw overboard.

Cardinal Wolsey continued, "Envious, malicious, and critical commentators, who are forever weak and deficient, often call our best accomplishments either not our accomplishments, or no accomplishments at all. Such commentators praise our worst deeds, which have a grosser quality, as being our best deeds.

"If we shall stand still out of fear that any action we take will be mocked or carped at, we would take root here where we sit, or sit as if we were only statues of statesmen."

King Henry VIII said, "Things done well and carefully exempt themselves from fear; the outcome of things done without a precedent is to be feared. Have you a precedent for this levy of taxes? I believe that there is not any.

"We must not rend our subjects from our laws, and stick them in our will. We must treat our subjects lawfully and not subject them to any unlawful whims.

"A sixth part of each person's wealth? That is a contribution to make one tremble! Why, if we take from every tree its small branches, bark, and part of its timber, although we leave it with a root, with the tree thus hacked, the air will drink the sap and the tree will die.

"To every county where this excessive tax is disputed, send our letters, giving free pardon to each man who has denied the force of this commission to levy excessive taxes.

"Be sure to look after it and do it. I give it to you — Cardinal Wolsey — to take care of."

Cardinal Wolsey said to his secretary, "Let me have a word with you."

He then said quietly so that no one but the secretary could hear him, "Let there be letters written to every shire about the King's grace and pardon. The aggrieved commoners harshly think of me. Let it be noised abroad that through our intercession this pardon and this repeal of the excessive taxes come."

Cardinal Wolsey used the royal plural — "our" — when talking to the secretary. He was careful not to do that when the King and Queen and other high-ranking people could hear him.

Cardinal Wolsey added, "I shall soon advise you further in the proceeding."

The secretary exited.

The Duke of Buckingham's former surveyor entered the room.

Queen Catherine said to King Henry VIII, "I am sorry that the Duke of Buckingham has incurred your displeasure."

"It grieves many people," King Henry VIII replied. "The Duke of Buckingham is a learned gentleman and a most marvelous speaker. No one is more indebted for having been born with good qualities. His education is such that he may prepare and instruct great teachers, and never seek for aid beyond himself.

"Yet it is important to note that when these so noble qualities shall prove not well directed, the mind growing once corrupt, they turn to vicious forms, ten times more ugly than they ever were beautiful. Noble qualities used to plan and perform evil actions become ugly.

"This man is so accomplished, and he was listed among wonders. We, almost with ravished listening, could listen to him talk for an hour and it was as if not even a minute had gone by.

"He, my lady, has used the graces that once were his in monstrous habits and given them monstrous appearances, and he has become as black as if he were besmeared in Hell.

"Sit by us; you shall hear — this man who is to give testimony about him was his trusted official — things about him to strike honor sad."

He ordered, "Tell the Duke of Buckingham's surveyor to recount the treacheries he has previously testified about. We cannot regard those treacheries as too little — lacking in loyalty and morality, and not deserving severe punishment — or hear too much about them."

Cardinal Wolsey said, "Stand forth, and with bold spirit relate the information that you, most like a concerned subject, have collected as evidence by watching the Duke of Buckingham."

"Speak freely," King Henry VIII ordered.

The Duke of Buckingham's former surveyor replied, "First, it was usual with him — every day it would infect his speech — that if the King should die without leaving behind a legitimate child, he would arrange things to make the scepter his. These very words I've heard him utter to his son-in-law, Lord Abergavenny. And to Lord Abergavenny he swore a menacing oath that he would get revenge upon the Cardinal."

Cardinal Wolsey said to King Henry VIII, "Please, your highness, note this part of his dangerous plan. His wish that you would die not having come true, his will is most malignant to your high person and it stretches beyond you, to your friends."

By "your friends," Cardinal Wolsey meant himself.

Queen Catherine said, "My learned Lord Cardinal, speak with Christian charity."

King Henry VIII said to the surveyor, "Speak on. On what grounds did he think he had a title to the crown if I should die without a legitimate child? Have you heard the Duke of Buckingham say anything about this point?"

The surveyor said, "He was brought to believe this by a vain prophecy of Nicholas Hopkins."

"Who is that Hopkins?" King Henry VIII asked.

The surveyor replied, "Sir, he is a Carthusian friar, the Duke of Buckingham's confessor, and he fed him every minute with words of sovereignty."

"How do you know this?" King Henry VIII asked.

The surveyor replied, "Not long before your highness traveled to France, while the Duke of Buckingham was at the Rose, his manor within the Saint Lawrence Poultney parish in London, the Duke asked what the Londoners were saying about the journey to France. I replied that men feared the French would prove to be perfidious, to the King's danger. Immediately, the Duke said, it was something to be feared, indeed, and he said that he feared it would prove the truth of certain words spoken by a holy monk 'who often,' he said, 'has sent messages to me, wishing me to permit John de la Car, my chaplain, at an appropriate time to hear from him in person about a matter of some importance. This monk made my chaplain swear under the seal of confession that he would utter to no living creature except to me, what the monk told him. Then, with solemn trust, the monk, with pauses, said that my chaplain should tell me, the Duke, that neither the King nor his heirs shall prosper. Tell him to strive to gain the love of the common people because the Duke shall govern England.'"

Queen Catherine said, "If I know you well, you were the Duke's surveyor, and you lost your office because of the complaints of the tenants. Take good care that you don't make charges against a noble person because of your anger — you will spoil your nobler soul. I say, take care. Yes, I heartily implore you to take care."

"Let him continue his testimony," King Henry VIII said.

He then ordered the surveyor, "Continue."

"On my soul, I'll speak nothing but truth," the surveyor said. "I told my lord the Duke that the monk might be deceived by the Devil's illusions and deceptions, and that it was dangerous for him to think about this so much that he believed the monk's prophecy, leading him — the Duke — to create some plot that was very likely to cause trouble. He answered, 'Tush, it can do me no damage.' He then added further that if the King had died as a result of his recent sickness, the Cardinal's and Sir Thomas Lovell's heads would have been cut off."

"Ha!" King Henry VIII said. "So foul? There's evil in this Duke of Buckingham."

He then asked the surveyor, "Can you say anything further?"

"I can, my liege."

"Proceed."

The surveyor began, "Being at Greenwich, after your highness had reproved the Duke about Sir William Blumer —"

King Henry VIII interrupted, "I remember that time. Sir William Blumer was my sworn servant, but the Duke retained him as his sworn servant. But go on. What happened then?"

The surveyor replied, "'If,' said the Duke, 'I for this act had been committed to prison, as to the Tower of London, I thought, I would have played the part my father meant to act upon the usurper King Richard III. When Richard III was at Salisbury, my father petitioned him to be allowed to come into his presence. If that petition had been granted, my father, pretending to show his loyalty by kneeling before Richard III, would have put his knife into him.'"

"A giant traitor!" King Henry VIII said.

Cardinal Wolsey said to Queen Catherine, "Now, madam, do you think his highness can live in freedom, with this Duke of Buckingham out of prison?"

"May God mend all!" Queen Catherine said.

"There's something more you want to say," King Henry VIII said to the surveyor. "What is it?"

"After the Duke talked about his father and the knife, he drew himself up to his full height, and with one hand on his dagger and the fingers of the other hand spread out on his breast, he raised his eyes and thundered a horrible oath, whose tenor was this: If he were ever evilly treated, he would outgo his father by as much as a performance does an irresolute purpose. His father had merely planned an assassination, but he would commit one."

Using the royal plural, King Henry VIII said, "There's the Duke of Buckingham's goal — to sheathe his knife in us. He has been arrested. Call him to an immediate trial. If he finds mercy in the law, it is his; if he can find no mercy in the law, then let him not seek mercy from us. By day and night, he's a traitor to the utmost height."

In a room of the palace in London, Lord Chamberlain and Lord Sands talked.

Lord Chamberlain asked, "Is it possible that the spells of France should trick men into such bizarre fashions?"

Lord Sands replied, "New customs, no matter how ridiculous — even unmanly and effeminate — yet are followed."

"As far as I can see," Lord Chamberlain said, "all the good our Englishmen have gotten by the recent voyage to France is merely a grimace or two of the face, but the grimaces are shrewd ones, for when our Englishmen hold them, you would swear immediately that their very noses had been counselors to the early French Kings Pepin or Clotharius, they keep so high up in the air."

Lord Sands said, "Our Englishmen all have new legs, and lame legs."

In this society, "to make a leg" meant "to bow." Lord Sands was complaining that many of the Englishmen who had recently traveled to France with the King had returned with a major case of Francophilia: love of France and of French ways. These Englishmen were walking and bowing in an affected French manner.

He continued, "One who had never seen them pace before would think that spavin and springhalt reigned among them."

Spavin and springhalt were diseases that affected horses' legs. A spavin was a tumor on a horse's leg. Springhalt was a disease that caused a horse's leg muscles to suddenly and involuntarily contract.

"By God's death!" Lord Chamberlain swore. "Their clothes are made after such a pagan cut, too, that surely they've worn out the fashions of all of the countries of Christendom."

Sir Thomas Lovell entered the room.

Lord Chamberlain asked, "How are you? What is the news, Sir Thomas Lovell?"

"Truly, my lord," Sir Thomas Lovell replied, "I hear of no news except for the new proclamation that's clapped upon the court gate."

"What is the proclamation about?" Lord Chamberlain asked.

"The reformation of our travelled gallants who fill the court with quarrels, talk, and tailors," Sir Thomas Lovell replied.

Quarrels — duels — were one of the fashions that these gallants had brought back from France.

Lord Chamberlain said, "I'm glad that the proclamation is there. Now I hope that our *monsieurs* will think that an English courtier may be wise, and yet never have seen the Louvre."

The plural of *monsieur* is *messieurs*, but Lord Chamberlain cared little about accuracy in such a matter.

Sir Thomas Lovell said, "They must leave those remnants of fool and feather and foolish fashions that they got in France, with all their honorable insistence on ignorance pertaining thereunto, as fights and fireworks, dueling and whoring, and abusing better men than they can be out of a foreign 'wisdom.'"

One of the more destructive customs the Englishmen had borrowed from France was a quickness to fight duels over what they considered points of honor. In this society, "fireworks" was a word used to refer to whores, especially whores who had a contagious venereal disease. In this society, syphilis was known as "the French disease."

He continued, "They must also renounce cleanly and wholly the faith they have in the French game of tennis, and tall stockings, short blistered breeches, and such other signs of travel, and stand under their legs again like honest men.

"If they don't do these things, then the alternative is, for so run the conditions of the proclamation, for them to pack off and return to their old playfellows in France.

"There in France, I take it, they may, *cum privilegio* — with immunity — wear away the reminder of their lewdness and be laughed at."

Lord Sands said, "It is time to give them medicine because their diseases have grown so contagious."

Lord Chamberlain said, "What a loss our ladies will have with the disappearance of these fine, pretty vanities!"

"That is true," Sir Thomas Lovell said. "There will be woe among the ladies indeed, lords. The sly bastards have got an effective and rapidly working trick to lay down ladies. A French song and a fiddle have no fellow — no equal — for getting the ladies in bed."

"May the Devil fiddle them!" Lord Sands said. "I am glad these Frenchified fellows are going, for, surely, there's no converting them back into Englishmen now. An honest country lord, as I am, beaten a long time out of play, may bring his plainsong and have an hour of hearing, and, by the Virgin Mary, have it held to be up-to-date music, too."

By "play," Lord Sands meant "playing music," but an eavesdropper may have also thought of "love playing."

Lord Chamberlain said, "Well replied, Lord Sands; your colt's tooth is not cast away yet."

The phrase "colt's tooth" meant "desire for wantonness."

"No, my lord," Lord Sands replied. "And it shall not be cast away, as long as I have a stump."

One meaning of "stump" is a rudimentary limb or member, and so the word "stump" can be used to refer to a penis. Of course, Lord Sands also meant "stump of a tooth."

Lord Chamberlain asked, "Sir Thomas, where were you going?"

"To Cardinal Wolsey's residence. Your lordship is a guest, too."

"Oh, it is true," Lord Chamberlain replied. "Tonight Cardinal Wolsey is hosting a supper, and a great one, for many lords and ladies. At the supper will be the beauty of this kingdom, I assure you."

Sir Thomas Lovell said, "That churchman bears a bounteous mind indeed. He has a hand as fruitful as the land that feeds us. His dews fall everywhere."

An eavesdropper might think that he had said about Cardinal Wolsey, "His dues fall everywhere."

Lord Chamberlain said, "There's no doubt that Cardinal Wolsey is noble. Anyone who says otherwise about him has a black and evil mouth."

"He can be bountiful, my lord," Lord Sands said. "He is wealthy; he has the wherewithal. For him, being miserly would show a worse sin than believing ill doctrine. Men of his way of life should be very liberal and generous. They are set here on Earth to serve as examples."

"True, they are indeed," Lord Chamberlain said. "But few now give such great suppers. My barge is waiting for me. Your lordship shall come along with me.

"Come, good Sir Thomas; otherwise, we shall be late, which I don't want to be because I was asked, along with Sir Henry Guildford, to be masters of ceremony this night."

Lord Sands replied, "I am your lordship's servant. I will do what you asked me to do."

In a hall in York Place, a small table had been placed under a canopy of state for Cardinal Wolsey. A longer table was for the guests. Anne Boleyn and several other ladies and gentlemen who were guests entered the hall.

Sir Henry Guildford, one of the masters of ceremony, also entered the hall.

Sir Henry Guildford said, "Ladies, a general welcome from his grace Cardinal Wolsey salutes you all; he dedicates this night to delightful pleasure and to you. No one here, he hopes, in all this noble bevy of ladies has brought with her one care or worry. Cardinal Wolsey wants all to be as merry as first good company and then good wine and good welcome can make good people."

Lord Chamberlain, Lord Sands, and Sir Thomas Lovell entered the hall.

Seeing Lord Chamberlain, Sir Henry Guildford said, "Oh, my lord, you're tardy. The very thought of this fair company clapped wings to me and made me hurry here."

"You are young, Sir Harry Guildford," Lord Chamberlain said.

Lord Sands said, "Sir Thomas Lovell, had the Cardinal only half my lay thoughts in him, some of these ladies would find a running banquet before they rested that I think would better please them."

"Lay" thoughts are unclerical, secular thoughts; for example, they could be thoughts about running after and laying the ladies.

A running banquet can be a light repast of sweets in between meals. "Running" is done in haste, and so perhaps Lord Sands was referring to a hasty bout of sweet, sweet lovemaking.

He added, "By my life, those ladies are a sweet society of beautiful ones."

Sir Thomas Lovell said, "Oh, that your lordship Cardinal Wolsey were now here to be confessor to one or two of these beautiful ladies!"

Lord Sands said, "I wish that I were their confessor. They would find easy penance."

"Indeed, how easy?" Sir Thomas Lovell asked.

Lord Sands replied, "As easy as a featherbed would afford it."

A confessor is a shriver, and a shift is a woman's undergarment. A joke of the time was to say that a woman had been "shriven to her shift" — that is, seduced.

Lord Chamberlain said, "Sweet ladies, will it please you to sit?

"Sir Harry, you sit the guests on that side; I'll take charge of this side.

"His grace is coming soon."

He said to two women, "No, you must not freeze. Two women placed together make cold weather."

He then said, "My Lord Sands, you are one who will keep them awake and lively. Please, sit between these ladies."

Lord Sands said, "By my faith, I thank your lordship.

"With your permission, sweet ladies, I will be seated between you. If I chance to talk a little wildly, forgive me. I got it from my father."

"Was he mad, sir?" Anne Boleyn asked.

"Oh, very mad, exceedingly mad. He was in love, too," Lord Sands said. "But he would bite no one. Just as I do now, he would kiss twenty of you with one breath."

He kissed Anne.

Lord Chamberlain said, "Well done, my lord.

"So, now you're fairly seated.

"Gentlemen, the penance lies on you, if these fair ladies leave here frowning tonight."

Lord Sands said, "Trust me, I will give the ladies a little cure for frowning."

Cardinal Wolsey entered the hall and sat in his chair of state.

He said, "All of you are welcome, my fair guests. Any noble lady, or gentleman, who is not freely merry is not my friend. To confirm my welcome to you, I drink this, and to you all, I wish good health."

He drank.

Lord Sands said, "Your grace is noble. Let me have such a bowl of wine as may hold my thanks, and save me so much talking. I will enjoy drinking my thanks to you."

A servant brought Lord Sands a bowl of wine.

Cardinal Wolsey said, "My Lord Sands, I am beholden to you. Cheer up your neighbors.

"Ladies, you are not merry.

"Gentlemen, whose fault is this?"

Lord Sands said, "The red wine first must rise in their fair cheeks, my lord, and then we shall have them talk to us so much that we gentlemen must be silent."

Anne Boleyn said, "You are a merry gamester, my Lord Sands."

By "gamester," she meant that he was a "merry fellow," but in his reply, he played on the meanings of "gamester" as "gambler" and "player in the game of love."

Lord Sands replied, "Yes, if I make my play."

A gambler who makes his play wins at a hand of cards. A lover who makes his play makes a successful attempt at seduction.

He added, "Here's to your ladyship."

He drank and then said, "Pledge it, madam. Drink, for it is to such a thing —"

Anne Boleyn bawdily joked, "You cannot show me your thing."

Lord Sands said, "I told your grace they would talk soon."

A drum and trumpet sounded, and guns fired.

"What's that noise?" Cardinal Wolsey asked.

Lord Chamberlain ordered, "Investigate, some of you."

A servant exited.

Cardinal Wolsey said, "What warlike noise is this, and for what purpose is it?

"No, ladies, don't be afraid. By all the laws of war, you're privileged. You will not be harmed."

The servant returned.

Lord Chamberlain asked, "Now, what is it?"

The servant replied, "A noble troop of strangers — for so they seem to be — have left their barge and landed. And they have come here, as if they were great ambassadors from foreign Princes."

Cardinal Wolsey said, "Good Lord Chamberlain, go and give them welcome — you can speak the French tongue. And, please, receive them nobly, and conduct them into our presence, where this Heaven of beauty shall shine at full blast upon them. Some of you go with him."

Lord Chamberlain and some servants exited.

Everyone stood up, and the tables were removed to make room for dancing.

Cardinal Wolsey said, "You have now an interrupted banquet, but we'll mend it. I wish a good digestion to you all, and once more I shower a welcome on you. All of you are welcome."

King Henry VIII and others entered, wearing masks and dressed like shepherds so that they would not be recognized. Ushered in by Lord Chamberlain, they went directly to Cardinal Wolsey and gracefully greeted him.

Lord Wolsey said, "A noble company! What are their pleasures?"

Lord Chamberlain said, "Because they speak no English, they asked me to tell your grace that, having heard by rumor that this so noble and so fair assembly would meet here this night, they could do no less out of the great respect they bear to beauty but leave their flocks and under your fair direction beg permission for them to view these ladies and entreat you to allow them to share an hour of revels with the ladies."

Cardinal Wolsey said, "Tell them, Lord Chamberlain, that they have done my poor house grace, for which I pay them a thousand thanks, and I ask them to please enjoy their pleasures here."

Cardinal Wolsey's male guests, including the new visitors, chose ladies for the dance. The disguised King Henry VIII chose Anne Boleyn to be his dance partner.

King Henry VIII said to Anne, "This is the fairest hand I ever touched! Oh, beauty, until now I never knew you!"

He had quickly forgotten his wife: Queen Catherine.

They danced.

Cardinal Wolsey said to Lord Chamberlain, "My lord!"

He replied, "Your grace?"

Cardinal Wolsey, who had a network of spies, which possibly may explain how he realized the new guests would speak French, said, "Please, tell them this from me: There should be one among them, by his person, who is more worthy of this seat of honor than myself. Also tell them that I would surrender this seat of honor to that person if I only knew which of them he was, out of my love and duty for him."

"I will, my lord," Lord Chamberlain said.

He whispered to the new, masked guests.

"What do they say?" Cardinal Wolsey asked.

Lord Chamberlain replied, "Such a one, they all confess, there is here indeed. They would have your grace find out who he is, and he will take the seat of honor."

"Let me see, then," Cardinal Wolsey said. "By all your good leaves, gentlemen; here I'll make my royal choice."

He correctly picked out King Henry VIII, who said, "You have found him, Cardinal."

King Henry VIII took off his mask and said, "You hold a fair assembly; you do well, lord. You are a churchman; if you weren't, I'll tell you, Cardinal, I should judge you now unfavorably."

He meant that a churchman such as a Cardinal was chaste and could refrain from the temptations of the female flesh around them.

Cardinal Wolsey replied, "I am glad that your grace is grown so merry and jolly."

"My Lord Chamberlain, please come here," King Henry VIII said. "Who is that beautiful lady I was dancing with?"

Lord Chamberlain replied, "If it please your grace, she is the daughter of Sir Thomas Boleyn — the Viscount Rochford — and she is one of Queen Catherine's ladies-in-waiting."

King Henry VIII said, "By Heaven, she is a dainty one."

He then said to Anne Boleyn, "Sweetheart, I would be unmannerly if I were to dance with you and not kiss you afterward, as is the custom."

He kissed her and said, "A health, gentlemen! Let it go round! Everyone, have a drink!"

Cardinal Wolsey asked, "Sir Thomas Lovell, is the banquet ready in the inner room?"

This banquet included fruit, candies, and wine.

Sir Thomas Lovell replied, "Yes, my lord."

Cardinal Wolsey said to the King, "Your grace, I fear, is a little heated from dancing."

"I fear, too much," King Henry VIII replied.

The heat came not just from dancing, but also from being around Anne Boleyn.

Cardinal Wolsey said, "There's fresher air, my lord, in the next chamber."

"Lead in your ladies, everyone," King Henry VIII said.

To Anne Boleyn, he said, "Sweet partner, I must not yet forsake you. Let's be merry."

He then said, "My good Lord Cardinal, I have half a dozen toasts to good health to drink to these fair ladies, and a dance to lead them once again, and then let's dream about who's best in favor."

He meant that they could dream about which lady was the most beautiful and about which gentleman was the favorite of the ladies.

He then said, "Let the music start up."

CHAPTER 2

— 2.1 —

Two gentlemen met on a street in Westminster.

The first gentleman asked, "Where are you going so quickly?"

"Oh, may God save you!" the second gentleman said, recognizing the first gentleman. "I am going to Westminster Hall to hear what shall become of the great Duke of Buckingham."

"I'll save you that labor, sir. All's now done, except for the ceremony of bringing back the prisoner."

"Were you there?"

"Yes, indeed, I was."

"Please, tell me what has happened," the second gentleman said.

"You may guess quickly what happened."

"Was he found guilty?"

"Yes, truly he was, and then he was condemned to die."

"I am sorry for it," the second gentleman said.

"So are a number of other people."

"But, please, tell me what happened during the trial."

"I'll tell you briefly," the first gentleman said. "The great Duke of Buckingham came to the bar, where to the accusations made against him he pleaded always not guilty and brought forth many acute arguments to refute the accusations. The King's attorney, who argued against the Duke, emphasized the depositions, testimony, and confessions of several witnesses, whom the Duke desired to have brought *viva voce* — with living voice; that is, in person — before him.

"At this, a number of people appeared against him: his surveyor; Sir Gilbert Peck, who is his Chancellor; John Car, his confessor; and that Devil-monk, Hopkins, who made this wickedness."

"Is Hopkins the man who fed the Duke with prophecies?" the second gentleman asked.

"The same. All these accused the Duke of Buckingham strongly, accusations that he gladly would have flung from him, but indeed he could not.

And so his peers, upon this evidence, have found him guilty of high treason. Much he spoke, and learnedly, to save his life, but everything he said either created ineffectual pity for him or was instantly disregarded."

"After all this, how did he bear himself? How did he act?"

"When he was brought again to the bar, to hear his knell rung out, his sentence, he was stirred with such an agony that he sweat extremely and spoke some things in anger that were ill and hasty. But he recovered his self-control, and sweetly in all the rest showed a most noble patience and calmness."

"I do not think he fears death," the second gentleman said.

"Surely, he does not. He never was so womanish as to fear death, but he may a little grieve because of the reason he will die."

"Certainly Cardinal Wolsey is the root cause of this."

"That is likely," the first gentleman said. "All surmises lead to that conclusion. First, Kildare, who was then the King's governor of Ireland, was condemned and lost his office and estate. After he was removed from office, the Earl of Surrey was sent to Ireland, and hastily, too, lest he should help his father-in-law: the Duke of Buckingham."

The second gentleman said, "That political trick was a deeply malicious one."

"Once the Earl of Surrey returns from Ireland, no doubt he will get payback for that political trick. It has been noted by everyone that for whomever the King favors, Cardinal Wolsey will immediately find employment elsewhere, and far enough from court, too, that he will not interfere with the Cardinal's influence over the King."

"All the commoners hate Cardinal Wolsey with deep loathing, and, I swear by my conscience, they would like to see him ten fathoms deep and drowned. In contrast, they love and dote on this Duke as much as they hate the Cardinal. They call the Duke bounteous Buckingham, the paragon of all courtly behavior —"

"Stop there, sir," the first gentleman said, "and see the noble ruined man you speak of."

The Duke of Buckingham entered, having left the court. Guards carrying staves tipped with metal walked before him. On each side of him were guards carrying halberds, weapons that are a combination of a battleax and a spear. The edge of each battleax was pointed toward the Duke of Buckingham, indicating that he had been sentenced to death by beheading. Accompanying the Duke of Buckingham were Sir Thomas Lovell, Sir Nicholas Vaux, Lord Sands, and several commoners.

The second gentleman said, "Let's stand quietly close by, and behold him."

The Duke of Buckingham, making a mighty effort to behave like a Christian despite the resentment he felt, said, "All good people, you who thus far have come to pity me, hear what I say, and then go home and forget me, know that I have this day received a traitor's sentence, and I must die with the name of traitor, yet I ask Heaven to bear witness that I am faithful and loyal to King Henry VIII, and I say that if I am not faithful and loyal to King Henry VIII, then if I have a conscience, let it sink me down to Hell, even as the axe falls!

"I bear the law no malice for my death. It has done, given the evidence and testimony presented to it, only justice.

"But those who sought this judgment against me I could wish were more Christian.

"Be they what they will, I heartily forgive them. Yet let them take care that they don't glory in evil deeds, nor build their evils on the graves of great men, for then my innocent, guiltless blood must cry out against them.

"I can never hope for further life in this world, nor will I plead for mercy, although the King has more mercies than I dare make faults. The King could, if he wished, pardon me, no matter what he thought I did.

"You few who have loved and respected me, and who dare to be bold enough to weep for me, Buckingham, are my noble friends and fellows, whom to leave is the only bitterness to me, the only dying.

"Go with me, like good angels, to my end, and as the long steel blade falls on me and divorces my soul from my body, make of your prayers one sweet sacrifice, and lift my soul to Heaven."

He then said to his guards, "Lead on, in God's name."

Sir Thomas Lovell said, "I beg your grace for charity. If ever any hidden malice in your heart were against me, now please forgive me frankly and freely."

The surveyor had testified that the Duke of Buckingham wanted to behead both Cardinal Wolsey and Sir Thomas Lovell.

The Duke of Buckingham replied, "Sir Thomas Lovell, I as freely forgive you as I would be forgiven. I forgive everyone. Out of all those numberless offences against me, there is none that I cannot make peace with: There is none that I cannot forgive. No black malice shall go with me to my grave.

"Commend me to his grace the King, and if he speaks of the Duke of Buckingham, please tell him that you met him when he was half in Heaven. My vows and prayers still are for the benefit of the King, and, until my soul forsakes and leaves my body, I shall cry for blessings upon him. May he live longer than I have time to count his years! May his rule be always beloved and loving! And when old Time shall lead him to his death, may goodness and he fill up one tomb!"

Sir Thomas Lovell said, "To the shore of the river, I must conduct your grace. Then I give my charge up to Sir Nicholas Vaux, who will take you to your place of death."

Sir Nicholas Vaux ordered some attendants, "Prepare everything. The Duke is coming. Make everything ready on the barge, and see that it is fitted with such things as suit the greatness of his person."

"No, Sir Nicholas," the Duke of Buckingham said, "let it alone. Recognition of my former great state now will but mock me. When I came here, I was the lord high constable and the Duke of Buckingham. Now, with my titles taken from me, I am only poor Edward Bohun. Yet I am richer than my base accusers, who never knew what truth and loyalty meant. I now seal my truth and loyalty with my blood as if I were sealing an official document, and with that blood I will make them one day groan for what they have done to me.

"My noble father, Henry of Buckingham, who first raised an army against the usurping Richard III, fled for aid to Banister, one of his servants. My father, who was distressed, was by that wretch betrayed, and he was executed without a trial. May God's peace be with him!

"King Henry VII succeeded Richard III. Truly pitying my father's loss, Henry VII, who was a most royal Prince and sovereign, restored me to my honors, and, out of ruins, made my name once more noble.

"Now his son, King Henry VIII, at one stroke has taken my life, honor, name, and all that made me happy forever from the world.

"I had my trial, and I have to say that it was a noble one, which makes me a little happier than my wretched father.

"Yet thus far my father and I are one in our fortunes. Both of us fell because of our servants, by those men we loved most — our servants gave us a most unnatural and faithless service!

"Heaven has a purpose in everything, yet you who hear me, regard as certainly true what I, a dying man, tell you: Where you are liberal and generous in your loves and counsels, be sure you are not loose and casual, for those loose and casual people you make friends and give your hearts to, when they once perceive the least obstacle in your fortunes, will fall away like water from you and never be found again except where they mean to sink you.

"May all good people pray for me! I must now leave you. The last hour of my long weary life has come upon me.

"Farewell. And when you would say something that is sad, talk about how I fell. I have finished, and may God forgive me!"

The Duke of Buckingham, his guards, and the other people accompanying him exited.

The first gentleman said, "Oh, this scene is full of pity! Sir, it calls, I fear, too many curses upon the heads of those who were the originators of the plot against the Duke of Buckingham."

"If the Duke is guiltless, then this scene is full of woe," the second gentleman said, "yet I can give you an inkling of an ensuing evil that if it happens it will be greater than this evil."

"May good angels keep it from occurring! What may it be? You do not doubt my trustworthiness, do you, sir?"

"This secret is so weighty that it will require a strong faith to conceal it."

"Tell it to me," the first gentleman said. "I do not talk much."

"I am confident that you are trustworthy, and I will tell it to you, I shall, sir. Didn't you recently hear gossip of a separation between the King and Catherine?"

"Yes, but the rumor didn't last, for when the King once heard it, out of anger he immediately sent a command to the Lord Mayor to stop the rumor, and quell those tongues that dared to disperse it."

"But that slander, sir," the second gentleman said, "is found to be a truth now, for it grows again fresher than it ever was, and people regard as certain that the King will venture to be separated from his wife. Either Cardinal Wolsey, or some person or people close to the King, have, out of malice to the good Queen, possessed him with a misgiving that will ruin her. In confirmation of this, too, Cardinal Campeius has recently arrived, and everyone thinks that he is here for this business."

"Cardinal Wolsey is behind this," the first gentleman said, "and his purpose is only to get revenge on the Holy Roman Emperor Charles V for not bestowing on him the Archbishopric of Toledo in Spain that he asked for."

"I think you have hit the mark. You are correct, but isn't it cruel that Queen Catherine should feel the pain of this? Cardinal Wolsey will get his revenge, and Queen Catherine must fall."

"It is woeful," the first gentleman said. "We are too open and exposed to talk about this matter here. Let's think and talk in private some more about this."

Lord Chamberlain read a letter out loud in an antechamber in the palace:

"My lord, concerning the horses your lordship sent for, with all the care I had I made sure that they were well chosen, broken in and trained, and equipped. They were young and handsome, and of the best breed in the north. When they were ready to set out for London, a man of Cardinal Wolsey's, by commission and brute force, took them from me, giving this reason: His master would be served before a subject, if not before the King. This stopped our mouths, sir.

"I fear Cardinal Wolsey will be served before a subject, if not before the King, indeed. Well, let him have them. He will have everything, I think."

The Duke of Norfolk and the Duke of Suffolk entered the antechamber.

The Duke of Norfolk said, "We are well met, my Lord Chamberlain."

"Good day to both your graces," Lord Chamberlain replied.

"How is the King employed?" the Duke of Suffolk asked. "What is he doing?"

"I left him in private," Lord Chamberlain said. "He was full of sad, serious thoughts and troubles."

"What's the cause?" the Duke of Norfolk asked. "What's the reason?"

"It seems the marriage with his brother's wife has crept too near his conscience," Lord Chamberlain said.

Before marrying King Henry VIII, Catherine had been married to his older brother. A Papal dispensation had allowed Henry VIII and Catherine to marry. King Henry VIII was now supposedly wondering whether his marriage was legitimate.

The Duke of Suffolk thought, *No, his conscience has crept too near another lady.*

The Duke of Norfolk replied to Lord Chamberlain, "That is true. This is Cardinal Wolsey's doing. He is the King-Cardinal. That blind priest, like the eldest son of Lady Fortune, turns the Wheel of Fortune just as he wishes."

Lady Fortune is often depicted as blind as she turns the Wheel of Fortune, improving some people's fortune in life, while worsening other people's fortune. Cardinal Wolsey was able to promote or demote people as he wished because King Henry VIII allowed him to have so much influence and power.

The Duke of Norfolk said, "The King will know what kind of man Cardinal Wolsey really is one day."

"I pray to God he does!" the Duke of Suffolk said. "King Henry VIII will never know himself otherwise. He will never act with the power of a King if Cardinal Wolsey continues to have so much influence over him and to wield so much of the King's power."

"How holily he works in all his business!" the Duke of Norfolk said sarcastically. "And with what zeal! Now that he has cracked the league between us and the Holy Roman Emperor Charles V, the Queen's great nephew, he dives into the King's soul, and there he scatters dangers, doubts, torturing of the conscience, fears, and despairs, and all these concerns and worries are all about his marriage. And to restore the King and do away with all of the King's concerns and worries, Cardinal Wolsey advises that the King divorce Queen Catherine. This would be a loss to the King of a woman who, like a jewel, has hung twenty years about his neck, yet never lost her luster. It would be a loss of a woman who loves him with that excellence that angels love good men with, even of her who, when the greatest blow of fortune falls, will bless the King. Isn't this advice of divorce 'pious'?"

"May Heaven keep me from such 'pious' counsel!" Lord Chamberlain said. "It is very true that this news is everywhere. Every tongue is speaking about a divorce, and every true heart weeps because of it. All who dare look into these affairs see this main outcome: Cardinal Wolsey wants King Henry VIII to marry the French King's sister. Heaven will one day open King Henry VIII's eyes that for so long have slept and not seen what a bold bad man Cardinal Wolsey really is."

"When that happens, King Henry VIII will free us from Cardinal Wolsey's slavery," the Duke of Suffolk said.

"We had better pray, and heartily, for our deliverance," the Duke of Norfolk said, "or this imperious man will work us all from Princes into pages. All men's honors lie like one lump of clay before him, to be fashioned into whatever rank — high or low — the Cardinal pleases."

"As for me, my lords," the Duke of Suffolk said, "I neither love the Cardinal nor fear him. There's my creed: As I am made without him, so I'll stand firm without him if the King will allow me to. Cardinal Wolsey's curses and his blessings affect me alike; they're breath I don't believe in — they are nothing but air. I knew him and I know him, and so I leave him to the man who made him proud: the Pope."

"Let's go in," the Duke of Norfolk said, "and with some other business distract the King from these sad thoughts that work too much upon him.

"My Lord Chamberlain, will you bear us company?"

"Excuse me," Lord Chamberlain said. "The King has sent me somewhere else. Besides, you'll find this a very bad time to disturb him. I wish health to your lordships."

"Thanks, my good Lord Chamberlain," the Duke of Norfolk said.

Lord Chamberlain exited, and the Duke of Norfolk and the Duke of Suffolk went to visit the King, who was reading.

The Duke of Suffolk said quietly about the King, "How sad he looks! Surely, he is much afflicted with worries."

King Henry VIII asked loudly, "Who's there?"

"I pray to God that the King is not angry at us," the Duke of Norfolk said.

"Who's there, I say?" King Henry VIII asked. "How dare you disturb my private meditations? Who do you think I am?"

The Duke of Norfolk replied, "We think you are a gracious King who pardons all offences in which malice was never intended. Our breach of duty here is business of state, in which we come to know your royal pleasure."

"You are too bold," King Henry VIII said. "I'll make you know the correct time for state business. Is this an hour for temporal affairs?"

Cardinal Wolsey and Cardinal Campeius entered the room. Cardinal Campeius held a commission from the Pope that allowed Cardinal Wolsey and himself to act in the matter of determining whether King Henry VIII's marriage to Queen Catherine was valid.

King Henry VIII said, "Who's there? My good Lord Cardinal? Oh, my Wolsey, you quiet my wounded conscience. You are a cure fit for a King."

He then said to Cardinal Campeius, "You're welcome, most learned reverend sir, in our Kingdom. Make use of us and it."

He then said to Cardinal Wolsey, "My good lord, take great care that I am not found to be just a talker."

In other words, he wanted Cardinal Wolsey to make sure that he, Henry VIII, carried out his welcome to Cardinal Campeius. A proverb of the time stated, "The greatest talkers are the least doers."

Cardinal Wolsey replied, "Sir, you cannot be found to be merely a talker; you are not capable of it. I wish that your grace would give us but an hour in private conversation."

King Henry VIII said to the Duke of Norfolk and the Duke of Suffolk, "We are busy; go."

The Duke of Norfolk whispered sarcastically to the Duke of Suffolk, "This priest has no pride in him."

The Duke of Suffolk whispered sarcastically to the Duke of Norfolk, "Not to speak of."

He added, without sarcasm, "I would not be so sick with pride even though it would get me Cardinal Wolsey's position. But this state of affairs cannot continue."

Norfolk whispered to Suffolk, "If it does, I'll venture one punch at the Cardinal."

Suffolk whispered to Norfolk, "And I will venture another."

The Duke of Norfolk and the Duke of Suffolk exited.

Cardinal Wolsey said to King Henry VIII, "Your grace has given a precedent of wisdom above all Princes in committing freely your scruple concerning the legitimacy of your marriage to the judgment of Christendom.

"Who can be angry now? What malice can reach you?

"Queen Catherine is the aunt of the Holy Roman Emperor Charles V, who is also the King of Spain. The Spaniards, tied blood and favor to her, must now confess, if they have any goodness, that the trial judging the legitimacy of your marriage is just and noble.

"All the clerics, I mean the learned ones, in Christian Kingdoms will have their free votes. Rome, the nurse of judgment, invited by your noble self, has sent one general tongue to us — one man to speak for all as spokesman. He is this good man, this just and learned priest, Cardinal Campeius, whom once more I present to your highness."

King Henry VIII said, "And once more in my arms I bid him welcome, and I thank the holy conclave for their loves for me. They have sent me such a man as I would have wished for."

Cardinal Campeius replied, "Your grace must necessarily deserve all foreigners' loves because you are so noble. To your highness' hand I tender my commission, by whose virtue, under the order of the court of Rome, you, my

Lord Cardinal Wolsey of York, are joined with me as Rome's servant in the impartial judging of this business."

"You are two fair and just men," King Henry VIII said. "The Queen shall be informed immediately why you have come.

"Where's Gardiner, my secretary?"

Cardinal Wolsey said, "I know your majesty has always loved Queen Catherine so dearly in your heart that you will not deny her what a woman of less position might ask for by law: scholars allowed freely to argue on her behalf."

"That is true," King Henry VIII said, "and she shall have the best, and I will give my favor to the scholar who represents her best. God forbid that I do otherwise. Cardinal, please call Gardiner, my new secretary, to come to me. I find that he is a fit fellow."

Cardinal Wolsey exited and quickly returned with Gardiner.

Cardinal Wolsey said quietly to Gardiner, "Give me your hand. I wish much joy and favor to you. You are the King's man now."

Gardiner said quietly to Cardinal Wolsey, "But I will always obey your commands because it is your hand that has raised me so high."

King Henry VIII said, "Come here, Gardiner."

The two talked quietly together.

Cardinal Campeius said quietly, "My Lord of York, wasn't there a Doctor Pace in this man's place as the King's secretary before him?"

"Yes, he was," Cardinal Wolsey said.

"Wasn't he regarded as a learned man?"

"Yes, certainly."

"Believe me, there's an ill opinion spread then about yourself, Lord Cardinal."

"What! About me?" Cardinal Wolsey said.

"They will not hesitate to say you envied Doctor Pace, and fearing that he would rise because he was so virtuous, you always kept him away from England on foreign business, which so grieved him that he became insane and died."

"May Heaven's peace be with him!" Cardinal Wolsey said. "That's enough Christian charity. Let's talk seriously. For living murmurers of gossip, there are places of rebuke where they can be punished. Doctor Pace was a fool, for he insisted on being virtuous.

"See Gardiner there? He's a good fellow and does whatever I command him to do. If he didn't, I would not allow him to be near either the King or me. Learn this, brother, we do not live to be touched in a familiar way by persons of low status."

King Henry VIII said to Gardiner, "Tell this with mildness to the Queen."

Gardiner exited.

King Henry VIII said, "The most convenient place that I can think of for such discussion of scholarly learning regarding my marriage is Blackfriars, where the Dominicans have a great hall. There you shall meet about this weighty business.

"My Wolsey, see that it is properly equipped.

"Oh, my lord, would it not grieve an able, sexually mature man to leave so sweet a bedfellow?"

The bedfellow may have been Queen Catherine, but it may have been Anne Boleyn.

The King continued, "But, conscience, conscience! Oh, it is a tender place; and I must leave her."

His conscience may have been the tender place, or the tender place may have been Queen Catherine's vagina.

Anne Boleyn and an Old Lady talked in an antechamber of Queen Catherine's apartments.

In the middle of a conversation, Anne Boleyn said, "Not for that neither. Here's the pang that torments: His highness having lived so long with her, and she so good a lady that no tongue could ever pronounce her dishonorable — by my life, she never knew harm-doing — now, after being enthroned for so many yearly courses of the Sun, still growing in majesty and pomp, to leave which is a thousand times more bitter than it is sweet at first to acquire, and after all this, the King orders her to go! The pity of this would move a monster."

The Old Lady said, "Hearts of the very hardest temper melt and lament for the Queen."

"Oh, God's will!" Anne Boleyn said. "It would be much better if she had never known pomp. Although pomp is secular and worldly, yet if that quarreler, Lady Fortune, divorces pomp from the bearer, it is as painful a suffering as that caused by the severing of soul and body."

"Alas, poor lady!" the Old Lady said. "She's a foreigner in England now again."

"So much the more must pity drop upon her," Anne Boleyn said. "Verily, I swear, it is better to be lowly born, and wander freely with humble livers in contentment and happiness, than to be perked up in a glittering grief, and wear a golden sorrow. It is better to be impoverished and happy than to be rich and unhappy."

"Our happiness is our best possession," the Old Lady said.

"By my truth and virginity, I would not be a Queen," Anne Boleyn said.

The word "Queen" was much pronounced much like the word "quean," which means "whore."

The Old Lady said, "Curse me, but I would, and I would risk maidenhead for it; and so would you, for all this taste of your hypocrisy. You, who have the so beautiful parts of a woman, have also a woman's heart, which has always desired eminence, wealth, and sovereignty, all of which, to say truly, are blessings, and which gifts, despite your hypocritical acting, the capacity of your soft cheveril conscience would receive, if you might please to stretch it."

Cheveril is soft, pliable leather used to make gloves. Fingers fit in gloves, and cheveril stretches so that the fingers fit. Penises fit in vaginas, and vaginas stretch so that the penises fit.

"No, truly," Anne Boleyn said.

"Yes, truly and truly," the Old Lady said. "Wouldn't you be a Queen?"

The Old Lady spoke unclearly; she may have said "quean," not "Queen."

"No, not for all the riches under Heaven," Anne Boleyn replied.

The Old Lady said, "It is strange: A bent coin worth only three pence would hire me, old as I am, to Queen [quean?] it, but, I ask you, what do you think of becoming a Duchess? Have you limbs that would bear that load of title?"

The way that Anne Boleyn would become a Duchess would be to marry a Duke. If that were to happen, Anne Boleyn would bear the Duke's weight on her limbs as they made love in the missionary position.

"No, truly," Anne Boleyn said.

"Then you are weakly made," the Old Lady said. "Pluck off a little."

"Pluck off a little" meant 1) "Come down in rank a little." That is, if you can't marry a Duke, then marry someone in the next lowest group: an Earl, and 2) "Take off some clothing." Besides the obvious meaning, the Old Lady had in mind that the length of the trains of dresses depended on the social status of the woman wearing the dress. Women of high social status had dresses with long trains. Women of lower social status had dresses with shorter trains.

The Old Lady continued, "I would not be a young Count in your way, for more than blushing comes to."

The Old Lady spoke unclearly, and she may have said "cunt" instead of "Count." If so, she had said, "I would not be a young cunt in your position, that of virginity, for more than blushing comes to." In other words, she would eagerly give up her virginity with no more cost than a blush.

The Old Lady continued, "If your back cannot vouchsafe — that is, bear — this burden, it is too weak ever to get — or beget — a boy."

Women who are unable to bear the weight of a man in the missionary position are unlikely to get married or to give birth to boys.

"How you do talk!" Anne Boleyn said. "I swear again that I would not be a Queen for all the world."

The Old Lady said, "Truly, for little England you would venture an emballing. I myself would for Carnarvonshire, even if there belonged no more to the crown but that."

"Little England" meant either 1) England, which is little compared to some other countries, or 2) "Little England" in Wales: the county of Pembrokeshire, whose inhabitants spoke English rather than Welsh.

"Emballing" meant 1) being invested with the ball — an emblem of royalty, and/or 2) being balled (the act of sex).

The Old Lady then said, "Look. Who is coming here?"

The Lord Chamberlain entered the antechamber and said, "Good morning, ladies. What would it be worth to know the secret of your conversation?"

Anne Boleyn replied, "My good lord, it is not even worth asking about. We were pitying the sorrows of our mistress the Queen."

Lord Chamberlain said, "Pitying the Queen's sorrows is a soft, tender business, and it is a suitable act for good women to do. There is hope that all will be well."

"I pray so to God, amen!" Anne Boleyn said.

"You have a kind, gentle mind, and Heavenly blessings follow such persons. So that you may, fair lady, perceive that I speak sincerely and that high note has been taken of your many virtues, the King's majesty commends to you his good opinion of you, and he gives to you honor that is no less flowing than the title of Marchioness of Pembroke. To this title he adds, out of his grace, a thousand pounds a year in annual support."

Anne Bolen replied, "I do not know what kind of my obedience I should tender; more than my all is nothing."

The Old Lady would know exactly how to thank the King: by giving him access to her vagina. Perhaps Anne Boleyn had some unconscious inkling of that. She was talking of giving the King more than all that she had, which is nothing. A man has a thing, or penis. A woman has no thing, or vagina.

Anne Boleyn continued, "My prayers are not words duly hallowed, and my wishes are not of more worth than empty vanities, yet prayers and wishes are all I can return to the King. I ask your lordship to please speak my thanks and my obedience, as from a blushing handmaid, to his highness the King, whose health and royalty I pray for."

In Genesis 16, Sarah, who is barren, sends her handmaid to have sex with Abram, Sarah's husband, so that he can have a child. Like Abram, King Henry VIII wanted to sire a male heir.

Lord Chamberlain replied, "Lady, I shall not fail to corroborate the fair opinion that the King has of you."

He thought, *I have perused her well. Beauty and honor in her are so mingled that they have caught the King, and who knows yet but from this lady may come a gem to lighten all of this isle?*

King Henry VIII and Anne Boleyn would be the parents of Queen Elizabeth I.

Lord Chamberlain said, "I'll go to the King, and say I spoke with you."

As he exited, Anne Boleyn said, "My honored lord."

The Old Lady said, "Why, look at this; see, see! I have been begging sixteen years in court, and I am still a beggarly courtier. I have never been able to find the right time — I was always either too early or too late — to make a successful petition for money. But you — oh, fate! I can't believe that you have had a fortune thrust upon you! You are a very fresh fish here, and yet you have had your mouth filled up before you open it!"

The Old Lady meant that Anne's "mouth" had been filled with money before she asked for it, but readers may be forgiven for thinking about sex, including oral sex — Anne's mouth could be filled with the King's penis before she opened it to say "I do" in the marriage ceremony.

Readers may also remember that in the future Anne Boleyn would be accused of adultery and treason, found guilty, and beheaded. The ancient Greeks and Romans put a coin in the mouth of a dead person so that the dead person's soul could pay a toll to Charon, who would ferry the soul to the Land of the Dead.

Anne Boleyn said, "This is strange to me."

The Old Lady asked, "How does it taste? Is it bitter? I'll bet forty pence that the answer is no. There was a lady once, it is an old story, she was a lady who would not be a Queen [quean?] — she would not be that for all the mud in Egypt. Have you heard that story?"

The story was actually recent. Anne Boleyn had very recently said that she would not be Queen for all the world.

Anne Boleyn said, "Come, you are pleasant. You are joking."

The Old Lady said, "If I had your reason for singing, I could soar higher than the lark. The Marchioness of Pembroke! A thousand pounds a year for pure respect! No other obligation! By my life, that promises more thousands. Like the trains of noble dresses, honor's train is longer than the front part of the skirt. By this time, now, I know your back will bear a Duchess. Tell me, aren't you stronger than you were?"

The Old Lady believed that Anne's back would bear the weight of a Duchess; that is, it would bear the weight — the guilt — of supplanting Queen Catherine, who had been married to King Henry VIII's older brother: Duke Arthur of Cornwall.

She was also asking whether Anne's back was strong enough to bear the weight of King Henry VIII and give birth to a son.

Anne Boleyn replied, "Good lady, make yourself mirthful with your own particular flights of fancy, and leave me out of them. If this had excited my passion even a jot, I would wish that I did not exist. I grow faint when I think about what follows.

"The Queen is comfortless, and we are forgetful in our long absence from her. Please, do not tell her what you've heard here."

"What do you think I am?" the Old Lady asked.

Readers may want to answer this question in this way: a bawd.

In a hall in Blackfriars, the inquiry regarding the legitimacy of the marriage of King Henry VIII and Queen Catherine was about to begin.

Trumpets and cornets sounded, and then a number of people in a procession entered the hall.

Two vergers, who carried short silver wands, entered the hall first. Vergers carry rods or wands before justices.

Two scribes, aka secretaries, wearing the academic robes of doctors of law, entered next.

The Bishop of Canterbury entered next.

The Bishop of Lincoln, the Bishop of Ely, the Bishop of Rochester, and the Bishop of Saint Asaph entered next.

A gentleman carrying the bag containing the Great Seal, and carrying a Cardinal's hat, entered next.

Two priests, each carrying a silver cross, entered next.

A bareheaded gentleman-usher, accompanied by a Sergeant-at-Arms bearing a silver mace, entered next.

Two gentlemen bearing two great silver pillars entered next.

Side by side, Cardinal Wolsey and Cardinal Campeius entered next.

Two noblemen with the sword and mace entered next.

King Henry VIII took a seat under the cloth of state — the canopy over the throne, which sat on a dais.

Cardinal Wolsey and Cardinal Campeius took seats at a lower level than the King. The two Cardinals would be judges.

Queen Catherine sat at some distance from King Henry VIII.

The Bishops placed themselves on each side of the court, in the manner of a consistory or ecclesiastical court of judgment.

On a lower level than the Bishops sat the scribes.

The lords sat next to the Bishops.

The rest of the attendants stood in convenient places about the hall.

Cardinal Wolsey said, "While our commission from Rome is read, let silence be commanded."

"What's the need for reading the commission out loud?" King Henry VIII said. "It has already publicly been read, and by all sides the authority of the commission has been recognized. You may, then, spare that time."

"Be it so," Cardinal Wolsey said. "Proceed."

A scribe said, "Say, King Henry VIII of England, that you are present in the court."

A crier repeated more loudly what the scribe had said.

"I am here," King Henry VIII said.

The scribe said, "Say, Queen Catherine of England, that you are present in the court."

The crier loudly repeated the words.

Queen Catherine made no answer; instead, she rose out of her chair, walked through the court to King Henry VIII, and knelt at his feet.

Then she said, "Sir, I desire that you do me right and justice, and I desire that you bestow your pity on me. I am a very poor woman, and I am a stranger who was not born in your dominions. I have here no impartial judge, and I have no assurance of equal, fair, and evenhanded friendship and proceeding.

"Sir, in what have I offended you? What cause has my behavior given to make you displeased with me that thus you should proceed to thrust me away from you and take your good grace from me? May Heaven witness that I have been to you a true and humble wife, at all times conformable to your will, always afraid to kindle your dislike. Yes, I have always been the obedient subject of your countenance, glad or sorry as I saw it inclined. When was the hour I ever contradicted your desire, or did not make it mine, too? Or which of your friends have I not striven to love, although I knew that that friend of yours were my enemy? What friend of mine have I had who brought down your anger on him have I continued to regard as my friend? I have not continued in my liking for such a person; instead, I gave notice to him that he was no longer my friend.

"Sir, call to mind that I have been your wife, your obedient wife, upward of twenty years, and I have been blessed with many children by you. If, in the course and process of this time, you can report, and prove it, too, anything against my honor, my bond to wedlock, or my love and duty, against your sacred person, then in God's name turn me away and let the foulest contemptible person shut the door against me, and so give me up to the sharpest kind of justice.

"If it please you, sir, King Henry VII, your father, was reputed to be a most prudent Prince and sovereign, of an excellent and unmatched intelligence and judgment. Ferdinand II, my father, the King of Spain, was reckoned to be one of the wisest Princes who there had reigned by many years before. It is not to be questioned that they had gathered a wise council to them from every realm, and they debated this business of whether a marriage between you and me would be legitimate. That wise council deemed our marriage lawful.

"Therefore, I humbly beg you, sir, to spare me until I may be advised by my friends in Spain, whose counsel I will ask for. If you will not grant my request, then in the name of God, may your pleasure be fulfilled!"

Cardinal Wolsey said, "You have here, lady, and of your choice, these reverend fathers. They are men of singular integrity and learning. Indeed, they are the best of the land, and they are assembled to plead your cause. It shall be therefore useless for you to wish to delay the work of this ecclesiastical court. Delaying will not make you feel quieter and calmer, and it will not rectify what is unsettling King Henry VIII."

Cardinal Compeius said, "His grace has spoken well and justly; therefore, madam, it's fitting that this royal court session proceed, and that, without delay, these reverend fathers' arguments be now produced and heard."

"Lord Cardinal Wolsey," Queen Catherine said, "to you I speak."

"What is your pleasure, madam?" Cardinal Wolsey replied.

"Sir, I am about to weep, but thinking that we are a Queen, or long have dreamed so, and knowing that I certainly am the daughter of a King, I'll turn my drops of tears into sparks of fire."

"Stay patient and calm," Cardinal Wolsey said.

"I will, when you are humble," Queen Catherine said. "No, I will be patient and calm before you are humble, or God will punish me."

She meant that Cardinal Wolsey would never be humble.

Queen Catherine continued, "I do believe, persuaded by potent circumstances, that you are my enemy, and I make my challenge that you shall not be my judge. I make my legal objection to you being my judge because it is you who have blown this coal into fire and caused this dissension between my lord — my husband — and me. May God's dew quench the fire that you started! Therefore, I say again, I utterly object, yes, from my soul, to you being my judge, and I refuse you as my judge. I say yet once more that I regard you as my most malicious enemy, and I do not think that you are at all a friend to truth."

Cardinal Wolsey replied, "I do profess that you are not speaking like yourself. You have always so far maintained Christian charity, and you have displayed the effects of a gentle disposition and of wisdom that surpasses what other women are capable of.

"Madam, you do me wrong. I have no anger against you, nor do I want injustice for you or for anyone. How far I have proceeded, or how much further I shall proceed, is warranted by a commission from the consistory, yes, the whole consistory of Rome.

"You charge against me that I have metaphorically blown this coal and caused dissension between the King and you. I deny it. The King is present. If it be known to him that I am denying that I did something that I really did, then he may wound, and worthily, my treachery! Yes, he may wound it as much as you have wounded my truth.

"If the King knows that I am guiltless of what you charge against me, then he knows that I am badly hurt by your false accusation. Therefore in him it lies to cure me, and the cure is to remove these thoughts from you. Before his highness speaks, I beg you, gracious madam, to take back what you said about me and to accuse me no more. Don't think such bad things about me."

"My lord, my lord," Queen Catherine said, "I am a simple woman, and I am much too weak to oppose your cunning. You're meek and humble-mouthed. You put on a full display of meekness and humility in order to advertise your place and calling, but your heart is crammed with arrogance, anger, and pride.

"You have, by Lady Fortune's and his highness' favors, gone lightly over low steps and now you have climbed high where powerful people are your servants, and your words, which are your servants, serve your will as it pleases you to pronounce their office. You order something to be done, and what you order is instantly done.

"I must tell you, you hold your secular reputation dearer than your high, spiritual profession. And I tell you again that I refuse to have you for my judge, and here, before you all, I say that I will appeal to the Pope to allow me to bring my whole case before his holiness so I can be judged by him."

She curtsied to King Henry VIII and started to exit.

Cardinal Compeius said, "The Queen is obstinate, antagonistic to justice, prompt to accuse it, and disdainful to be tried by it. It is not well. She's going away."

King Henry VIII ordered, "Call her again."

The crier said loudly, "Queen Catherine of England, come into the court."

Queen Catherine's gentleman-usher, whose name was Griffith, said to her, "Madam, you are called back to the court."

"What need have you to pay attention to that?" Queen Catherine said. "Please, keep moving out of the court with me. When *you* are called, then *you* return. Now, may the Lord help me because they vex me past my patience! Please move on. I will not stay here, no, nor will I ever again upon this business make my appearance in any of their courts."

Queen Catherine and her attendants exited.

King Henry VIII said, "Go on your way, Kate. Any man in the world who shall report he has a better wife, let him be trusted in nothing because he spoke falsely when saying that. If your splendid qualities, sweet gentleness, saint-like meekness, wife-like self-control, obedience to me while giving commands to others, and your supreme and pious qualities could speak out for you, they would say that you, alone, are the Queen of Earthly Queens.

"She's nobly born, born noble, and like her true nobility, she has conducted herself nobly towards me."

Cardinal Wolsey said, "Most gracious sir, in humblest manner I request of your highness that it shall please you to declare, in the hearing of all these ears — for where I am robbed and bound, there I must be unloosed, although there I cannot be immediately and fully compensated for what has been done to me — whether I ever broached this business to your highness, or laid any difficulty or doubt concerning your marriage in your way, which might induce you to question whether your marriage is legitimate. Also say whether I have to you, except with giving thanks to God for such a royal lady, spoken the least word that might be to the prejudice of her present state, or stain of her good person."

King Henry VIII said, "My Lord Cardinal Wolsey, I excuse you; yes, upon my honor, I free you from that accusation. You already know that you have many enemies who don't know why they are your enemies, but who, similar to village curs, bark when their fellows do. By some of these, the Queen has been made angry. You are excused."

King Henry VIII turned to the other people in the court and said, "But do you want to hear more exoneration for Cardinal Wolsey than those few words? Let me say more.

"Cardinal Wolsey, you have always wished the sleeping of this business; you have never desired it to be stirred up, but often you have hindered — often, I say — the passages made toward it.

"People in the court, on my honor, I speak for my good Lord Cardinal Wolsey on this point, and thus far clear him.

"Now, to tell you what moved me to hold this court to determine whether my marriage to Catherine is legitimate, I will be bold with your time and your attention: Pay attention as I describe what induced me to do this. Thus it came; give heed to it.

"My conscience first received a tenderness, misgiving, and prick, upon hearing certain speeches uttered by the Bishop of Bayonne, who was then the French ambassador. He had been sent here while we were discussing a marriage between the Duke of Orleans and our daughter, Mary.

"In the discussion of this business, before we made a decision, he — I mean the Bishop — required a respite during which he might inform the King his lord whether our daughter, Mary, was legitimate. He needed to do this because Mary was the child of my marriage with the dowager who was formerly my brother's wife.

"This respite shook the heart of my conscience and entered me — yes, with a power as if I had been impaled with a spit — and made my chest tremble. This respite forced its way into my conscience, resulting in bewildered considerations thronging against me and pressing me to exercise caution.

"First, I thought I stood not in the smile of Heaven, which had commanded Nature that my lady's womb, if it conceived a male child by me, should do no more offices of life to it than the grave does to the dead. I thought this because my lady's male children were either stillborn or died shortly after being born and coming into the air of this world.

"Therefore, I took thought and concluded that this was a judgment on me, that my Kingdom, which was very worthy to have the best heir of the world, would not be made glad by me because Heaven and Nature were against me producing such an heir.

"Then I weighed the danger that my realms stood in because of my failure to produce a living male heir, and that gave to me many a groaning pain. Thus hulling in the wild sea of my conscience, I steered towards this remedy."

"Hulling" means for a ship to have furled sails while on the sea; in this culture, a ship that is hulling cannot be steered.

King Henry VIII continued, "The remedy I mean is this for which we are now present here together. That's to say, I meant to rectify my conscience. Previously, I felt very sick, and even now I don't feel well. All the reverend fathers of the land and learned doctors of law will give me my remedy by determining whether my marriage to Queen Catherine is legitimate.

"First I began in private with you, my Lord Bishop of Lincoln. You remember how under my oppression I sweat, when I first raised this issue with you."

"I remember very well, my liege," the Bishop of Lincoln replied.

"I have spoken for a long time," King Henry VIII said. "Please say yourself to what extent you satisfied me."

"So please your highness," the Bishop of Lincoln said, "the question at first so staggered me — because it was a question of such mighty moment and its outcome was something to be feared — that I made myself doubt the most daring counsel that I had and I entreated your highness to take this course of action that you are taking here."

The most daring counsel was perhaps a recommendation of a divorce between the King and the Queen.

King Henry VIII said, "I then raised this issue with you, my Lord Bishop of Canterbury, and I got your permission to make this present summons of the Queen to this court.

"I left no reverend person unsolicited in this court, but by individual and particular consent I proceeded under your hands and seals. I got your written permission to hold this ecclesiastical court.

"Therefore, let us go on. Not because of any dislike in the world against the person of the good Queen, but only because of the sharp, thorny points of the reasons I have told you, I have taken this action.

"If you prove that the marriage of my Queen and me is lawful, then by my life and Kingly dignity, I say that I am contented to spend the rest of my mortal existence with her, Catherine our Queen, rather than with even the most excellent woman who is considered to be the paragon of the world."

Cardinal Compeius said, "So please your highness, the Queen being absent, it is necessary and fitting that we adjourn this court until a later day.

"Meanwhile, an earnest attempt must be made to the Queen to persuade her to call back the appeal she intends to make to his holiness the Pope."

King Henry VIII thought, *I can perceive that these Cardinals are trifling with me. I abhor this dilatory sloth and these tricks of Rome.*

My learned and well-beloved servant, Thomas Cranmer, please return. I know that when you arrive here, my comfort comes with you.

He said out loud, "Dissolve and break up the court. I say, let us move on."

CHAPTER 3

— 3.1 —

Queen Catherine and her female attendants were sewing in a room of her apartment.

Queen Catherine said to one of her female attendants, "Take up your lute, girl. My soul grows sad with troubles. Sing, and disperse them, if you can. Stop working."

The female attendant sang this song:

"Orpheus with his lute made trees,

"And the mountain tops that freeze,

"Bow themselves when he did sing:

"To his music plants and flowers

"Ever sprung; as if Sun and showers

"There had made a lasting spring.

"Every thing that heard him play,

"Even the billows of the sea,

"Hung their heads, and then lay by and rested.

"In sweet music is such art,

"Mortal worry and grief of heart

"Fall asleep, or hearing, die."

A gentleman entered the room.

Queen Catherine asked, "What is it?"

The gentleman replied, "If it pleases your grace, the two great Cardinals are waiting for you in the reception chamber."

"Do they wish to speak with me?" Queen Catherine asked.

"They wanted me to say so, madam," the gentleman replied.

"Ask their graces to come here," Queen Catherine ordered.

The gentleman exited.

Queen Catherine said, "What can their business be with me, a poor weak woman, who has fallen from favor? I do not like their coming. Now I think about it, the Cardinals should be good men, and their business should be as righteous as the Cardinals are good, but not all hoods make monks."

Cardinal Wolsey and Cardinal Campeius entered the room.

"Peace to your highness!" Cardinal Wolsey said.

"Your graces find me here doing a part of the work of a housewife," Queen Catherine said. "I should learn to do all the work of a housewife as preparation for the worst that may happen. Perhaps I will be cast out of the palace with nothing and will have to work to make my living.

"What is your business with me, reverend lords?"

Cardinal Wolsey said, "If it would please you, noble madam, to withdraw into your private chamber, we shall tell you the full reason for our coming to visit you."

"Tell me here," Queen Catherine said. "There's nothing I have done yet, on my conscience, that deserves a corner in which it can hide."

A proverb stated, "Truth seeks no corners."

She continued, "I wish that all other women could say this with as free and innocent a soul as I do!

"My lords, I am so much happier than many others that I don't care if my actions were to be tried by every tongue, if every eye saw them, and if malice and base gossip were set against them. I know that my life is constantly upright.

"If your business concerns me and my situation as wife to King Henry VIII, then say so — out with it boldly. Truth loves open dealing."

Cardinal Woolsey, who did not want the female attendants to know what he, Cardinal Campeius, and Queen Catherine would be discussing, said, "*Tanta est erga te mentis integritas, regina serenissima —*"

This Latin meant, "So great is the integrity of my purpose towards you, most serene Queen —"

Queen Catherine, who was not serene, objected, "Oh, my good lord, no Latin. I am not such a truant since my coming to England from Spain as not to know the language of the country I have lived in so long. A strange — foreign — tongue makes my matter of concern seem stranger — more suspicious.

"Please, speak in English. Here among us are some who will thank you, if you speak the truth, for their poor mistress' sake. Believe me, she has suffered much wrong done to her, Lord Cardinal.

"The most deliberate sin I have ever yet committed may be absolved in English."

"Noble lady," Cardinal Wolsey said, "I am sorry my integrity — and my service to his majesty and, um, to you — should breed such deep suspicion, where only loyalty was meant.

"We come not to accuse you of anything. We don't want to taint that honor of yours that every good tongue blesses, nor do we want to betray you in any manner to sorrow — you already have too much sorrow, good lady. Instead, we have come to find out what you think about the weighty difference between the King and you, and we have come to declare, like magnanimous and honorable men, our just opinions about your court case. We hope to comfort you."

Cardinal Campeius said, "Most honored madam, my Lord Cardinal Wolsey of York, out of his noble nature, zeal, and obedience he always has borne your grace, forgetting like a good man your recent condemnation both of his truth and himself, a condemnation that went too far, offers, as I do, as a sign of peace, his service and his counsel."

Queen Catherine thought, *Yes, they offer their service and counsel in order to betray me.*

She said out loud, "My lords, I thank you both for your good wills. You speak like honest men; I pray to God that you prove to be honest men!

"But I truly don't know how to make you an impromptu answer in such a serious matter that is so near my honor — and even nearer to my life, I fear — with my weak intelligence, and to such men of gravity and learning."

This culture regarded men as being more intelligent than women.

Queen Catherine continued, "I was seated and at work among my ladies-in-waiting, and I was very little, God knows, expecting either such men as you or such business as this. For the sake of the woman whom I have been — for I feel that these are the final hours and the death spasm of my greatness as Queen — I ask your good graces to let me have time and counsel for my case. Alas, I am a woman who is friendless and hopeless!"

Cardinal Wolsey said, "Madam, you wrong the King's love with these fears. Your hopes and friends are infinite."

Queen Catherine said, "In England I have few hopes and few friends for my benefit. Can you think and believe, lords, that any Englishman would dare to give me counsel or be a known friend to me, against his highness' pleasure, even if he has grown so desperate as to be honest and truthful, and yet still live as a subject to the King?

"No, truly, my friends — those who must compensate for my afflictions, and those whom I have grown to trust — do not live here in England. They are, as are all my other comforts, far from here and in my own country of Spain, lords."

Cardinal Campeius said, "I wish that your grace would set aside your griefs, and take my counsel."

"How can I do that, sir?" Queen Catherine asked.

He replied, "You can put yourself under the King's protection. He's loving and very gracious, and it will be much better both for your honor and yourself, for if the trial of the law overtakes you, you'll depart from here disgraced."

"He tells you rightly," Cardinal Wolsey said.

This was a threat. If she agreed to a divorce, she would retain some honor and be treated well as the dowager of King Henry VIII's older brother — her marriage to Arthur, the older brother, was regarded by all as legitimate. But if she did not agree to the divorce and a trial was held with acrimonious judges, she could end up severely disgraced. In addition, her enemies were powerful, and one possible outcome if she continued to resist could be being accused of adultery and treason, followed by a beheading.

Queen Catherine replied, "You tell me what both of you wish for — my ruin. Is this your Christian counsel to me? Get out! Heaven is still above all of us; in Heaven a Judge sits Whom no King can corrupt."

"Your rage misjudges us," Cardinal Campeius said.

"Your actions shower all the more shame on you," Queen Catherine said. "Upon my soul, I thought that you were holy men. I thought that you were two reverend personifications of the cardinal virtues.

"But I fear that you are two personifications of cardinal sins — and of hollow hearts."

The cardinal sins are the seven deadly sins: pride, greed, envy, wrath, sloth, gluttony, and lechery. The cardinal virtues are justice, prudence, temperance, and fortitude. In addition, there are three Heavenly graces, aka virtues: faith, hope, and love/charity.

Queen Catherine continued, "Mend your hollow hearts, for shame, my lords. Is this your Christian comfort for me? Is this the cordial — the medicinal drink — that you bring a wretched lady, a woman lost among you, laughed at, scorned?

"I will not wish you half my miseries because I have more charity than that, but say that I warned you. Take heed, for Heaven's sake, take heed, lest one day the burden of my sorrows suddenly falls upon you."

Cardinal Wolsey said, "Madam, this is purely a frenzy of yours. The good we offer to you, you misconstrue as malice."

"You turn me into nothing," Queen Catherine said. "Woe upon you and all such false professors of the Christian faith! Would you have me — if you have any justice, any pity; if you are anything but the mere appearance of churchmen — put my sick self into the hands of one who hates me?

"Alas, the King has already banished me from his bed. His love was too long ago! I am old, my lords, and all the fellowship I hold now with the King my husband is only my obedience. What can happen to me above this wretchedness? All your efforts have made me accursed like this."

"Your fears are worse than the reality," Cardinal Campeius said.

Queen Catherine replied, "Have I lived thus long — let me speak for myself, since virtue finds no friends — as a wife, a true and loyal and faithful wife? I dare say without vainglory that I am a woman who never has been branded with suspicion of adultery. Haven't I with all my full affections always met the King's wishes? Haven't I always loved him second only to Heaven? Haven't I always obeyed him? Haven't I always, out of fondness and love for him, almost idolized him? Haven't I almost forgot my prayers in my attempt to make him happy? And am I thus rewarded?

"This treatment of me is not good, lords. Bring me a woman who has been constantly loyal to her husband, one who never dreamed of a joy beyond his pleasure, and compared to that woman, when she has done the most and the best she can do, yet I will add an honor: a great patience."

"Madam, you wander from the good we aim at," Cardinal Wolsey said.

"My lord, I dare not make myself so guilty as to give up willingly that noble title your master — the King — wed me to. Nothing but death shall ever divorce my dignities."

"Please, listen to me," Cardinal Wolsey said.

Queen Catherine said, "I wish that I had never trod on this English earth, or felt the flatteries that grow upon it! You have angels' faces, but Heaven knows your hearts."

A proverb stated, "Fair face, foul heart."

She continued, "What will become of me, a wretched lady, now! I am the unhappiest woman living."

She said to her ladies-in-waiting, whose fortunes were connected to hers, "Alas, poor women, where are now your fortunes! I am shipwrecked upon a Kingdom where I have no pity, no friend, no hope, and no kindred to weep for me, and where almost no grave is allowed me. Like the lily that once was mistress of the field and flourished, I'll hang my head and perish."

Psalm 103:15-16 states, "*The days of man are as grass: as a flower of the field, so flourisheth he. For the wind goeth over it, and it is gone, and the place thereof shall know it no more*" (1599 Geneva Bible).

Cardinal Wolsey said, "If your grace could but be brought to know our ends are honest, you would feel more comfort. Why should we, good lady, for what reason should we wrong you? Alas, our positions and the way of our religious calling are against it. We are to cure such sorrows, not to sow them.

"For goodness' sake, consider what you are doing, how you may hurt yourself, yes, utterly grow away from the King's acquaintance, by this behavior.

"The hearts of Princes kiss obedience, so much they love it, but to stubborn spirits the hearts of Princes swell, and grow as terrible as storms."

Again, this was a threat. Bad things could happen to Queen Catherine if she continued to resist agreeing to a divorce.

Cardinal Wolsey continued, "I know you have a gentle, noble temperament, a soul as calm as a sea with no wind and waves. Please, think that we are what we profess to be: peacemakers, friends, and servants."

Cardinal Campeius said, "Madam, you'll find that this is true. You wrong your virtues with these weak women's fears. A noble spirit, like yours that was put into you when you were conceived, always casts such doubts, as if they were false coin, from it.

"The King loves you. Be careful that you don't lose his love. As for us, if you please to trust us in your business, we are ready to use our utmost efforts in your service."

Queen Catherine said, "Do what you will, my lords, and please forgive me if I have behaved without good manners. You know I am a woman who lacks the intelligence to make a seemly, decorous answer to such persons as yourselves.

"Please, pay my respects to his majesty. He has my heart still, and he shall have my prayers as long as I live. Come, reverend fathers, bestow your counsels on me. She — I — now begs, who little thought, when she set foot on England here, she should have bought her dignities at such an expensive price."

This sounds as if she capitulated, yet history records that she continued to refuse to appear in any court that discussed the legality of her marriage to King Henry VIII.

The Duke of Norfolk, the Duke of Suffolk, the Earl of Surrey, and Lord Chamberlain talked together in an antechamber leading to King Henry VIII's apartment. The Earl of Surrey was the Duke of Buckingham's son-in-law; he had been in Ireland when the Duke of Buckingham was found guilty of treason and beheaded.

The Duke of Norfolk said, "If you will now unite in your complaints, and press them with steadfastness, Cardinal Wolsey cannot resist them. If you neglect the opportunity we have at this time, I cannot promise anything except that you shall sustain more disgraces to add to these you bear already."

The Earl of Surrey said, "I am joyful to have the least opportunity that may recall to my mind my father-in-law, the Duke of Buckingham, and let me be revenged on the person who caused his death."

The Duke of Suffolk asked, "Which of the nobles have not been despised by Cardinal Wolsey, or at least have not been coldly ignored as if they were a stranger? When did he regard and respect the stamp of nobleness in any person other than himself?"

Lord Chamberlain said, "My lords, you speak what you please. I know what Cardinal Wolsey deserves from you and me, but I very much fear what could happen if we do something to him, although now the time gives an opportunity to us. If you cannot bar his access to King Henry VIII, never attempt to do anything against Cardinal Wolsey, for his tongue has a kind of witchcraft over the King. Cardinal Wolsey is very persuasive and can make the King do what Cardinal Wolsey wants him to do."

"Oh, don't fear Cardinal Wolsey doing that," the Duke of Norfolk said. "His ability to influence the King is gone. The King has found evidence against him that forever mars the honey of the Cardinal's language. No, Cardinal Wolsey is firmly fixed in the displeasure of the King."

The Earl of Surrey said, "Sir, I would be glad to hear such news as this once every hour."

"Believe it because it is true," the Duke of Norfolk said. "In the divorce of King Henry VIII and Queen Catherine, Cardinal Wolsey acted contrary to the wishes of the King. This has all been unfolded to the King, and now Cardinal Wolsey is in such a position as I would wish my enemy to be."

"How did Cardinal Wolsey's intrigue come to light?" the Earl of Surrey asked.

"Very strangely," the Duke of Suffolk said.

"How?" the Earl of Surrey asked.

The Duke of Suffolk replied, "Cardinal Wolsey's letters to the Pope miscarried and came to the eye of the King. In those letters, the King read that against his wishes the Cardinal was entreating his holiness the Pope to delay the judgment of the divorce. In a letter, Cardinal Wolsey wrote that if the divorce did take place, '*I perceive that my King is entangled in affection to a lady-in-waiting of the Queen's: Lady Anne Boleyn.*'"

"Does the King have this letter?" the Earl of Surrey asked.

"Believe it," the Duke of Suffolk replied.

"Will the Cardinal's treachery work?" the Earl of Surrey asked.

"The King by reading this letter perceives clearly how Cardinal Wolsey moves in a devious, roundabout way but always follows his own course. But in this point all of the Cardinal's tricks flounder, and he brings his medicine after his patient's death: The King has already married the fair lady."

"I wish that were true!" the Earl of Surrey said.

"May you be happy in your wish, my lord," the Duke of Suffolk said, "for, I profess, you have it. Your wish has come true."

"Now, may all my joy follow from this conjunction — this marriage!" the Earl of Surrey said.

"I add my 'amen' to that!" the Duke of Suffolk said.

"All men say 'amen' to that!" the Duke of Norfolk said.

"The order has been given for her coronation," the Duke of Suffolk said. "By the Virgin Mary, this order is newly given, and it ought to be left untold to some ears. But, my lords, she is a splendid woman, and she is perfect in mind and features. I believe that from her will fall some blessing to this land, which shall be remembered forever on account of it."

"But will the King read and then tolerate and ignore this letter of the Cardinal's?" the Earl of Surrey asked. "The Lord forbid!"

"By the Virgin Mary, amen to that!" the Duke of Norfolk said. "The Lord forbid!"

"No, no, the King will not tolerate it," the Duke of Suffolk said. "There are other wasps that buzz about the King's nose that will make this wasp sting all the sooner. Cardinal Campeius has stolen away to Rome. He has taken no official leave, and he has left the law case of the King's divorce unfinished. He was sent speedily to Rome as the agent of our Cardinal Wolsey to advance Cardinal Wolsey's plots. I assure you that the King cried out in disgust and anger when he learned all this."

Lord Chamberlain said, "May God now further cause him to be angry and let him cry out in disgust and anger all the more loudly!"

"But, my lord, when does Thomas Cranmer return?" the Duke of Norfolk asked. "He has been traveling around, gathering learned opinions about whether the King is justified in divorcing Queen Catherine."

"He has returned in the form of a report of his opinions, which have satisfied the King that his divorce is justified. These opinions are those of Cranmer together with almost all the famous colleges in Christendom. Shortly, I believe, King Henry VIII's second marriage shall be publicly proclaimed, and her coronation shall be held. Catherine no more shall be called Queen; instead, she will be called Princess Dowager and widow to Prince Arthur, the King's older brother."

The Duke of Norfolk said, "This Cranmer is a worthy fellow, and he has taken much pain to do the King's business."

"He has," the Duke of Suffolk said, "and we shall see him rewarded for it by being made an Archbishop. He shall be made the Archbishop of Canterbury."

"So I hear," the Duke of Norfolk said.

"It is true," the Duke of Suffolk said. "It will happen."

He looked up and said, "The Cardinal!"

Cardinal Wolsey and Cromwell, his servant, entered the room. They were at a distance from the others and did not see them for a while.

The Duke of Norfolk said, "Look. Look. The Cardinal is moody."

Cardinal Wolsey said, "The packet of letters, Cromwell. Did you give it to the King?"

"I handed it to the King himself, in his bedchamber," Cromwell replied.

"Did he look inside the packet?"

"Immediately, he unsealed the letters and the first letter he viewed, he did so with a serious mind; his face showed that he was paying careful attention to the letter. He then ordered that you wait for him here this morning."

Cardinal Wolsey asked, "Is he ready to come out of his apartment?"

"I think that by this time he has left his apartment," Cromwell replied.

"Leave me alone for a while," Cardinal Wolsey ordered.

Cromwell exited.

Cardinal Wolsey thought, *It shall be to the Duchess of Alençon, the French King's sister. Henry VIII shall marry her. Anne Boleyn! No! I'll have no Anne Boleyns for him! There are more important things than a fair face. Boleyn! No, we'll have no Boleyns. I hope to hear quickly from Rome. The Marchioness of Pembroke!*

One of Anne Boleyn's titles was the Marchioness of Pembroke.

The Duke of Norfolk said, "Cardinal Wolsey is unhappy."

The Duke of Suffolk said, "Maybe he has heard that the King whets his anger toward him."

"May the King's anger be sharp enough, Lord, for Your justice!" the Earl of Surrey said.

Cardinal Wolsey thought, *Anne Boleyn is the recent Queen's gentlewoman, a knight's daughter. Should she be her mistress' mistress! Should she be the Queen's Queen! This candle does not burn clearly. It is I who must snuff it. Then out it goes."*

The candle is the marriage of Anne Boleyn to King Henry VIII. It was not burning brightly yet, Cardinal Wolsey thought, because Anne Boleyn's marriage to King Henry VIII had not yet taken place. It was up to him to snuff the candle. The snuff of the candle is the partially consumed wick. To keep the candle burning brightly, the candle must occasionally be snuffed, meaning that the wick must be trimmed. But to snuff a candle has another meaning: to put out the candle.

King Henry VIII had wanted Cardinal Wolsey to snuff the candle: to clear away the obstacles to his marriage to Anne Boleyn. But Cardinal Wolsey wanted to snuff the candle: to prevent the King from marrying Anne.

Cardinal Wolsey thought, *What though I know her to be virtuous and well deserving? Yet I know her to be a passionate Lutheran, and not beneficial to our cause, that of Roman Catholicism and our plan for King Henry VIII to marry the sister of the King of France, and so she should not lie in the bosom of our*

"He is vexed at something," the Duke of Norfolk said.

"I hope that it is something that will fret the string — the master-cord — of his heart!" the Earl of Surrey said. "I hope it cuts the Cardinal's heartstring, and he dies!"

King Henry VIII entered the room, reading a paper. Sir Thomas Lovell accompanied him.

"The King! The King!" the Duke of Suffolk said.

King Henry VIII said, "What piles of wealth has Cardinal Wolsey accumulated to his own possession! And what prodigal expenditures each hour seem to flow from him! How, in the name of thrift, does he rake all this money and these possessions together when he has such high expenses! Now, my lords, have you seen Cardinal Wolsey?"

The Duke of Norfolk pointed to the Cardinal and replied, "My lord, we have stood here observing him. Some strange commotion is in his brain: He bites his lip, and startles, stops suddenly, looks upon the ground, lays his finger on his temple, immediately springs out into a fast gait, stops again, strikes his breast hard, and casts his eye upward to the Moon. We have seen him act very strangely."

"It may well be that a mutiny is in his mind," King Henry VIII said. "This morning he sent me state papers to peruse, as I had ordered him, and do you know what I found there — on my conscience, put there unwittingly?

"Truly, I found an inventory that listed the many pieces of his silver plate and gold plate, his treasure, rich fabrics, and household ornaments, which I find to have such value that it far exceeds what a subject of mine ought to possess."

"It's Heaven's will," the Duke of Norfolk said. "Some spirit put this paper in the packet to bless your eye with. Heaven wanted you to find and read that inventory of Cardinal Wolsey's possessions."

King Henry VIII looked at Cardinal Wolsey and said, "If we thought that he was contemplating Heavenly matters — matters that are above the Earth — and if we thought that his attention was fixed on spiritual objects, we would allow him to continue to dwell in his musings, but I am afraid his thoughts are about things below the Moon, things that are not worth his serious consideration."

King Henry VIII sat down and whispered to Sir Thomas Lovell, who went over to Cardinal Wolsey and brought him out of his deep thoughts.

Startled, Cardinal Wolsey said, "Heaven forgive me!"

He went to the King and said, "May God for ever bless your highness!"

"My good lord," King Henry VIII said, "you are full of Heavenly stuff, and bear in your mind the inventory of your best graces, which you were just now running over. You scarcely have time to steal from spiritual leisure a brief span to keep your Earthly audit. To be sure, in that I deem you to be an ill manager of your Earthly affairs, and because of it I am glad to have you be my companion."

The King was mocking Cardinal Wolsey by using such Earthly terms as "stuff," "inventory," "steal," "leisure," and "audit." The Heavenly audit, as opposed to an Earthly audit, is the audit that takes place on the Day of Judgment.

Cardinal Wolsey replied, "Sir, for holy offices I have a time. I also have a time to think upon the part of the business that I bear in the state, and Nature requires her times of rest and preservation, which necessarily I, her frail son, like my mortal brothers, must tend to."

"You have spoken well," King Henry VIII said.

"And may your highness always yoke together, as I will lend you reason to do, my doing well with my saying well!" Cardinal Wolsey said.

"You have said well again," King Henry VIII said. "And it is a kind of good deed to say well, and yet words are no deeds."

A proverb states, "Saying is one thing, doing another." Another proverb states, "From words to deeds is a great space."

King Henry VIII continued, "My father loved you. He said he did, and his *said* he *did*, and with his deed he crowned his word upon you. Ever since I have had my office as King of England, I have kept you near my heart; I have not only employed you where high profits might come home to you, but I have pared and reduced my own possessions in order to bestow my bounties upon you."

Suspicious, Cardinal Wolsey thought, *What does this mean?*

The Earl of Surrey thought, *May the Lord promote this business!*

King Henry VIII continued, "Have I not made you the prime, most important man of the state?"

As Lord Chancellor, one of his many titles, Cardinal Wolsey was second only to the King.

King Henry VIII continued, "Please, tell me if what I just now said you have found to be true. And, if you may confess it, say in addition whether you are indebted to us or not. What do you say?"

"My sovereign," Cardinal Wolsey said, "I confess that your royal graces, which have been showered on me daily, have been more than my deliberate efforts can repay, although my deliberate efforts have exceeded the endeavors of all other men. My endeavors have always come up too short compared to my desires, although they have kept pace with my abilities: I have done all I can and yet not accomplished what I hoped. My own ends have been mine to the extent that they always pointed to the good of your most sacred person and the profit of the state: I have subordinated my own profit in order to profit you and England. For your great graces that you have heaped upon me, a poor undeserver, I can render nothing but my faithful and allegiant thanks, my prayers to Heaven for you, and my loyalty, which always has and always shall be growing until the winter that is death shall kill it."

"You have answered fairly," King Henry VIII said. "A loyal and obedient subject is therein illustrated in your words. The honor of it pays the act of it, as in the contrary the foulness is the punishment."

A proverb states, "Virtue is its own reward." In other words, the intrinsic quality of honor is the reward of being virtuous.

King Henry VIII continued, "I presume that, as my hand has opened bounty to you, my heart dropped love, my power rained honor, more on you than on any other, so your hand and heart, your brain, and every function of your power, should — even though your bond of duty is, as it were, in love's particular — be more to me, your friend, than to any other. You have the duty of a subject to your King, and a subject should love his King, but since I am your personal friend, you also have the bond of personal friendship to me, your King, and personal friendship carries its own duties with it."

Cardinal Wolsey said, "I profess that for your highness' good I have always labored more than for my own. What is my own? It is that *am, have,* and *will-be.* My own is what I am, what I have, and what I will be."

Cardinal Wolsey most valued power and money, and what he hoped his *will-be* would be was a powerful man who had much wealth. He was honest about what is *his own*.

He continued, "Though all in the world should split asunder their duty to you, and throw it from their soul, and though perils did abound, as thick as thought could make them and appear in forms more horrid, yet my duty, as does a rock against the tumultuous flood, should the approach of this wild river withstand, and stand unshaken yours."

"It is nobly spoken," King Henry VIII said. "Take notice, lords, he has a loyal breast, for you have seen him open it."

He then handed Cardinal Wolsey two papers and said, "Read over this paper, and after reading it, read this other paper, and then go to breakfast with what appetite you have."

King Henry VIII frowned at Cardinal Wolsey and then exited. Smiling and whispering to each other, the nobles in the room exited behind him.

Cardinal Wolsey said to himself, "What does this mean? What sudden anger is this? How have I reaped it? He departed frowning from me, as if ruin leaped from his eyes. So looks the enraged lion at the daring huntsman who has wounded him, and then the lion makes him nothing — the lion obliterates him."

"I must read this paper. I fear it contains the story behind his anger."

He read the paper and said, "It is so. This paper has ruined me. It is the account of all that world of wealth I have drawn together for my own ends — indeed, to become Pope, and pay my friends in Rome.

"Oh, this is negligence fit for a fool to fall by. What perverse Devil made me put this major secret in the packet I sent the King? Is there no way to cure this? No new trick to beat this paper away from his brains? I know it will stir him strongly, yet I know a way that, if it succeeds, will spite bad fortune and get me out of this mess."

He looked at the other paper and said, "What's this? '*To the Pope*'! This letter, as I live, has all the business I wrote to his holiness the Pope. So then, farewell! I have touched the highest point of all my greatness, and, from that full meridian of my glory, I hasten now to the setting of my greatness. I shall fall like a bright meteor in the evening, and no man shall see me anymore."

The Duke of Norfolk, the Duke of Suffolk, the Earl of Surrey, and Lord Chamberlain returned.

The Duke of Norfolk said, "Hear the King's pleasure, Cardinal Wolsey. He commands you to render up the Great Seal immediately into our hands, and to confine yourself to Asher House, the residence of my Lord of Winchester, until you hear further from his highness."

"Stop," Cardinal Wolsey said. "Where's your commission, lords? Where are your written orders for me to hand over the Great Seal? Words cannot carry authority so weighty; a written commission is needed for so important a matter."

The Duke of Suffolk said, "Who dares to oppose words bearing the King's will when those words come directly and expressly from the King's mouth?"

Cardinal Wolsey replied, "Until I find more than will or oral words to hand over the Great Seal — I mean by 'will' your malice, you officious lords — know that I dare and I must deny to do it.

"Now I feel of what coarse metal and mettle you are molded — it is malice. How eagerly you follow my disgraces, as if it fed you! And how sleek and wanton you appear in everything that may bring my ruin!

"Follow your vindictive courses of action, men of malice. You have 'Christian' warrant for them, and, no doubt, in time will find their 'fit' rewards.

"The King, who is my and your master, entrusted that Great Seal that you ask for with such violence to me with his own hand. He told me to enjoy it, with the official position of Lord Chancellor and attendant honors, during my life. And, to confirm his goodness, he ratified his entrusting the Great Seal to me with letters-patents, aka public documents. Now, who'll take it from me?"

The Earl of Surrey replied, "The King, who gave it to you, will take it from you."

"He himself must do it, then," Cardinal Wolsey said.

Now the Earl of Surrey and Cardinal Wolsey began to use insulting pronouns such as "thou," "thy," and "thee" to refer to each other In this culture, these words were not insulting to use when speaking to intimates such as friends, wives, or children, or when speaking to servants, but they were insulting in this situation.

"Thou are a proud traitor, priest," the Earl of Surrey said.

Cardinal Wolsey replied, "Proud lord, thou lie. Within these past forty hours, the Earl of Surrey would have preferred to burn his tongue than to say so."

"Thy ambition, thou scarlet sin, robbed this bewailing land of noble Buckingham, my father-in-law," the Earl of Surrey said.

As a Cardinal, Wolsey wore scarlet clothing.

The Earl of Surrey was alluding to Isaiah 1:18: "*Come now, and let us reason together, saith the Lord: though your sins were as crimson, they shall be made white as snow: though they were red like scarlet, they shall be as wool*" (1599 Geneva Bible).

The Earl of Surrey continued, "The heads of all thy brother Cardinals, with thee and all thy best parts bound together, were not worth a hair of his. A plague on your political maneuverings!

"You sent me to be Governor of Ireland, far from my father-in-law's succor, far from the King, and far from all who might have mercy on the crime thou attributed to him, while your great goodness, out of holy pity, absolved him with an axe by cutting off his head."

Cardinal Wolsey said, "This, and everything else this talking lord can lay upon my reputation, I answer is most false. The Duke of Buckingham by law found his deserts. How innocent I was from any private malice in his death, his noble jury and foul crimes can witness.

"If I loved many words, lord, I should tell you that you have as little honesty as honor, that in the way of loyalty and truth toward the King, my ever royal master, I dare match myself with a sounder man than Surrey can be and than all who love Surrey's follies can be."

The Earl of Surrey said, "By my soul, your long Cardinal's coat, priest, protects you; otherwise, thou should feel my sword in thy life-blood.

"My lords, can you endure to hear this arrogance? And from this fellow?"

A servant could be called "fellow," but in this context the word "fellow" was insulting.

The Earl of Surrey continued, "If we live thus tamely, to be thus jaded — deceived — by a piece of scarlet, then farewell to our nobility. Let his grace go forward, and dazzle us with his cap like trappers dazzle larks."

People would use a piece of bright scarlet cloth — or a mirror — to lure and fascinate larks and then throw a net over them.

The Earl of Surrey was also alluding to Joan Lark, Cardinal Wolsey's mistress.

Cardinal Wolsey said, "All goodness is poison to thy stomach."

The Earl of Surrey said, "Yes, that 'goodness' of gleaning all the land's wealth into one heap, into your own hands, Cardinal, by extortion and misuse of your official position. Yes, that 'goodness 'of your intercepted packets of letters you wrote to the Pope against the interests of the King. Your 'goodness,' since you provoke me, shall be very notorious and widely known.

"My Lord of Norfolk, as you are truly noble and as you respect the common good, the state of our despised nobility, our male children, who, if Cardinal Wolsey continues to live, will scarcely be gentlemen, much less inherit the titles of Earl and Duke from their fathers, produce now the grand sum of Cardinal Wolsey's sins, the articles of indictment collected from his life.

"I'll startle you worse than the sacring bell did when the brown wench lay kissing in your arms, Lord Cardinal."

The sacring bell rang to let people know it was time to go to prayers.

As a priest, Cardinal Wolsey was supposed to be celibate, but it was widely known that he was not.

A brown wench is a lower-class woman. Upper-class women protected their skin from the Sun.

Cardinal Wolsey said, "How much, I think, I could despise this man, except that I am bound in Christian charity against it!"

The Duke of Norfolk said to the Earl of Surrey, "Those articles, my lord, are in the King's own hand; he has possession of them. But I can tell you this much, the articles of indictments are for foul crimes."

Cardinal Wolsey replied, "So much fairer and spotless shall my innocence arise, when the King knows my truth and loyalty."

The Earl of Surrey replied, "This cannot save you. I thank my memory that I still remember some of these articles, and they shall be widely known. Now, if you can blush and cry 'guilty,' Cardinal, you'll show a little honesty."

"Speak on, sir," Cardinal Wolsey said. "I defy your worst objections. If I blush, it is because I see a nobleman who lacks manners."

"I had rather lack manners than my head," the Earl of Surrey said. "Listen to the charges against you!

"First, that without the King's assent or knowledge, you contrived to be a Papal legate, by which power you maimed the jurisdiction of all the Bishops in England."

The Duke of Norfolk said, "Second, that in all you wrote to Rome, or to foreign Princes, '*Ego et Rex meus*' — 'I and my King' — was always inscribed, in which you put yourself first and described the King as your servant."

The Duke of Suffolk said, "Third, that without the knowledge either of King or council, when you went as an ambassador to the Holy Roman Emperor Charles V, you made bold to carry into Flanders the Great Seal, which is not permitted to leave England."

If the Great Seal were to fall into the wrong hands, forged letters stamped with the Great Seal could greatly embarrass the King.

The Earl of Surrey said, "Fourth, that you sent a large commission of delegates to Gregory de Cassado, to conclude, without the King's will or the state's permission, a treaty between his highness and the Duke of Ferrara, Italy."

Gregory de Cassado was the English ambassador to the Papal court. Ferrara was a city-state in Italy.

The Duke of Suffolk said, "Fifth, that out of sheer ambition, you have caused your profile and holy hat to be stamped on the King's coin."

The Earl of Surrey said, "Sixth, that you have sent uncountable wealth — by what means acquired, I leave to your own conscience — to supply Rome, and to bribe your way to honors, to the complete undoing of all the Kingdom of England. Many more there are, which since they are about you, and odious, I will not taint my mouth by enumerating them."

Lord Chamberlain said, "Oh, my lord, do not press a falling man too far! It is a virtue not to. Cardinal Wolsey's faults, sins, and crimes lie open to the laws; let the laws, not you, correct him. My heart weeps to see him have now so little of his formerly great self."

"I forgive him," the Earl of Surrey said.

The Duke of Suffolk said, "Lord Cardinal Wolsey, because all of those things you have done recently by your power as a Papal legate within this kingdom, fall into the compass of a *praemunire* — our English law against preempting and denying the King's authority by asserting Papal jurisdiction in England — the King's further pleasure is that therefore this writ be sued against you: You must forfeit all your goods, lands, tenements, castles and chattels, and whatsoever else, and be out of the King's protection and declared an outlaw. This is my charge."

The Duke of Norfolk said, "And so we'll leave you to your meditations about how to live better. As for your stubborn answer about the giving back of the Great Seal to us, the King shall know it, and, no doubt, shall 'thank' you. So fare you well, my little-good Lord Cardinal Wolsey."

They exited, leaving Cardinal Wolsey alone.

"So farewell to the little good you bear me," Cardinal Wolsey said. "Farewell! A long farewell to all my greatness! This is the state of man: Today he puts forth the tender leaves of hopes; tomorrow he blossoms and bears his blushing honors thick upon him; on the third day comes a frost, a killing frost; and when he, good and easygoing man, thinks that most certainly his greatness is ripening, the killing frost nips his root, and then he falls, as I do.

"I have ventured, like little carefree, playful boys who swim with the aid of bladders filled with air, these many summers in a sea of glory, but I went far beyond my depth. My high-blown pride at length broke under me and now has left me, weary and old with service, to the mercy of a turbulent stream that must forever hide me.

"Vain pomp and glory of this world, I hate you. I feel my newly opened heart. Oh, how wretched is that poor man who hangs on Princes' favors! There is, between that smile we would aspire to, that sweet aspect of Princes, and the ruin Princes cause, more pangs and fears than wars or women have. And when that poor man who hangs on Princes' favors falls, he falls like Lucifer, never to hope again."

Psalm 118:9 states, "*It is better to trust in the Lord, than to have confidence in princes*" (1599 Geneva Bible).

Isaiah 14:12 states, "*How art thou fallen from heaven, O Lucifer, son of the morning? and cut down to the ground, which didst cast lots upon the nations?*" (1599 Geneva Bible).

Cromwell, Cardinal Wolsey's servant, entered the room. He was in a state of shock.

"Why, how are you now, Cromwell?" Cardinal Wolsey asked.

"I have no power to speak, sir," Cromwell replied.

"What, are you amazed at my misfortunes? Can your spirit wonder that a great man should decline? If you weep, I know that I have indeed fallen."

"How is your grace?"

"Why, well," Cardinal Wolsey replied. "I have never been so truly happy, my good Cromwell. I know myself now; and I feel within me a peace above all Earthly high official positions; I have a still and quiet conscience. The King has cured me, for which I humbly thank his grace, and from these shoulders of mine, these ruined pillars, out of pity, he has taken a load that would sink a navy — the load of too much honor. Oh, it is a burden, Cromwell, it is a burden too heavy for a man who hopes for Heaven!"

"I am glad your grace has made that right use of it," Cromwell said. "I am glad that your grace has been able to learn a moral lesson from what has happened to you."

"I hope I have," Cardinal Wolsey said. "I am able now, I think, out of a fortitude of soul I feel, to endure more miseries and greater miseries by far than my weak-hearted enemies dare give to me.

"What is the news going around?"

"The heaviest and the worst is your falling out of favor with the King."

"God bless him!" Cardinal Wolsey said.

"The next important piece of news is that Sir Thomas More has been chosen Lord Chancellor in your place."

"That's somewhat quick," Cardinal Wolsey said, "but he's a learned man. May he continue long in his highness' favor, and do justice for truth's sake and his conscience; may his bones, when he has run his course of life and sleeps in blessings, have a tomb with orphans' tears wept on them!"

The Lord Chancellor was the official guardian of orphans. If he did his job well, orphans would mourn his death.

"What other news?" Cardinal Wolsey asked.

"Cranmer has returned with welcome, and he has been installed Lord Archbishop of Canterbury."

"That's news indeed."

Cromwell said, "The last piece of news is that the Lady Anne, whom the King has secretly been long married to, this day was viewed in open as his Queen, going to chapel. People now talk only about her coronation."

"There was the weight that pulled me down," Cardinal Wolsey said. "Oh, Cromwell, the King has gotten the better of me. I have lost forever all my glories because of that one woman. No Sun shall ever usher forth my honors, or gild again the noble troops who waited on me and wanted me to smile.

"Go, get away from me, Cromwell. I am a poor fallen man, unworthy now to be your lord and master. Seek the King — that Sun, I pray, may never set! I have told him who you are and how true and loyal you are. He will promote you. Some little memory of me will stir him — I know his noble nature — and he will not let your promising service perish, too, as he has mine. Good Cromwell, do not neglect the King. Take this opportunity now, and provide for your own future safety."

"Oh, my lord, must I, then, leave you?" Cromwell said. "Must I necessarily forego so good, so noble, and so true and loyal a master? Bear witness, all of you who don't have hearts of iron, with what sorrow Cromwell leaves his lord. The King shall have my service, but my prayers forever and forever shall be yours."

"Cromwell, I did not think I would shed a tear in all my miseries, but you have forced me, because of your honest truth and loyalty, to play the woman and cry. Let's dry our eyes, and thus far hear me, Cromwell, and, when I am forgotten, as I shall be, and sleep in dull cold marble, where no mention of me more must be heard, say that I taught you — say that Wolsey, who once trod the ways of glory, and sounded all the depths and shoals of honor, found for you a path, out of his wreck, to rise in, a sure and safe path, although your master missed it.

"Note carefully my fall and what ruined me. Cromwell, I charge you to fling away ambition. Because of the sin of ambition, the angels fell; how can Man, then, the image of his Maker, hope to profit by it?

"Love yourself last. Cherish the hearts of those who hate you. Corruption does not profit more than honesty. Always in your right hand carry gentle peace that will silence envious tongues. Be just, and fear not. Let all the ends you aim at be your country's, your God's, and truth's; then if you fall, Cromwell, you fall as a blessed martyr!

"Serve the King, and — please, lead me in. There take an inventory of all I have, to the last penny. It is the King's now. My Cardinal's robe and my integrity to Heaven are all I dare now to call my own.

"Oh, Cromwell, Cromwell! Had I but served my God with half the zeal I served my King, He would not in my old age have left me naked and defenseless to my enemies."

"Good sir, have patience," Cromwell said.

"So I have," Cardinal Wolsey said. "Farewell to the hopes of court! My hopes in Heaven do dwell."

CHAPTER 4

— 4.1 —

Two gentlemen met each other on a street. The coronation of Queen Anne Boleyn at Westminster Abbey was taking place that day, and she and a procession would pass along this street after she left Westminster Abbey.

"You're well met once again," the first gentleman said.

"So are you," the second gentleman replied.

"Have you come to take your stand here, and see the Lady Anne pass from her coronation?"

"Yes, that is why I am here today. The last time we met, the Duke of Buckingham came this way from his trial."

"That is very true, but that time offered sorrow. This time offers general joy."

"That is good," the second gentleman said. "The citizens, I am sure, have shown fully their devotion to royalty — as, to give them their due, they are always ready to do — in celebration of this day with shows, pageants, and sights of honor."

"These shows, pageants, and sights of honor have never been greater, nor, I assure you, better appreciated, sir."

"May I be bold and ask what that paper in your hand contains?"

"Of course," the first gentleman said. "It is the list of those who claim their offices and duties this day by custom of the coronation.

"The Duke of Suffolk is the first, and his claim is to be the High Steward."

The High Steward presides over the coronation.

The first gentleman continued, "Next is the Duke of Norfolk, and his claim is to be the Earl Marshal."

The Earl Marshal arranges great ceremonies.

The first gentleman continued, "You may read the rest."

"I thank you, sir," the second gentleman said. "If I had not known those customs, I should have been indebted to your paper.

"But, I ask you, what's become of Catherine, the Princess Dowager? How goes her business — the matter concerning her?"

The first gentleman said, "That I can tell you, too. The Archbishop of Canterbury, accompanied with other learned and reverend fathers of his order, held a recent court at Dunstable, six miles off from Ampthill, where the Dowager Princess resided. She was often summoned by them to appear at the court, but she did not appear. And, to be short, because of her non-appearance and the King's recent worry that he may not be legally married to her, by the majority assent of all these learned men she was divorced from the King. After that judgment was made, she moved to Kimbolton, where she remains now. She is sick."

"I pity the good lady," the second gentleman said.

Trumpets sounded.

The second gentlemen said, "Listen! The trumpets sound. Stand close by because the Queen is coming."

This is the order in which the procession of the coronation passed by the two gentlemen:

1. Trumpeters appeared first and blew a lively flourish.

2. Two judges appeared.

3. The Lord Chancellor appeared, with his mace of office and the bag containing the Great Seal carried before him.

4. Singing choristers appeared with playing musicians.

5. The Mayor of London appeared, bearing the mace. Just behind him was the Garter King of Arms, in his coat of arms, and on his head a gilt copper crown.

6. The Marquess Dorset appeared, bearing a scepter of gold and wearing on his head a demi-coronal of gold. With him appeared the Earl of Surrey, carrying a rod of silver with a dove and crowned with an Earl's coronet. They were wearing collars made of S's joined together.

7. The Duke of Suffolk appeared, wearing his robe of state, with his coronet on his head, bearing a long white wand, in his office as High Steward. With him appeared the Duke of Norfolk, carrying the rod of a Marshal and wearing a coronet on his head. They were wearing collars made of S's joined together.

8. Four people representing the Cinque-ports — ports on the southeast coast of England — appeared, holding a canopy. Under the canopy was Queen Anne, wearing her robe and with her hair richly adorned with pearls and crowned. At her sides walked the Bishops of London and Winchester.

9. The old Duchess of Norfolk appeared, wearing a coronal of gold, wrought with flowers, carrying Queen Anne's train.

10. Certain ladies or Countesses, wearing plain circlets of gold without flowers, appeared.

The two gentlemen talked about the members of the procession as they passed by them.

The second gentleman said, "This is a royal procession, believe me. These people I know, but who is that man who is carrying the scepter?"

"He is the Marquess Dorset," the first gentleman said, "and the man carrying the rod is the Earl of Surrey."

"He is a bold, brave gentleman. I suppose that this man is the Duke of Suffolk?"

"Yes, that is he. He is acting as the High Steward today."

"And is that man my Lord of Norfolk?" the second gentleman asked.

"Yes," the second gentleman replied.

He then looked at Queen Anne and said, "May Heaven bless you! You have the sweetest face I ever looked on."

He then said to the first gentleman, "Sir, as I have a soul, she is an angel. Our King has all the riches of the Indies in his arms, and more and richer, when he embraces that lady. I cannot blame his conscience."

The second gentleman thought that King Henry VIII's conscience might be bothering him because he had had to divorce his first wife, Catherine, in order to marry Anne Boleyn, but Queen Anne was so beautiful that the second gentleman could not blame the King for divorcing Catherine.

The first gentleman said, "Those who carry the cloth of honor — the canopy — over her are four barons of the Cinque-ports."

"Those men are happy; and so are all men who are near her," the second gentleman said. "I take it that the woman who carries the train of the Queen's robe is that old noble lady, the Duchess of Norfolk."

"It is; and all the rest are countesses."

"Their coronets say so," the second gentleman said. "These are stars indeed, and sometimes falling ones."

He was punning. One meaning of "falling" was "yielding her virginity."

The first gentleman said, "No more of that."

The procession exited. Trumpets sounded, and a third gentleman joined the first two gentlemen. The third gentleman was obviously hot; he was sweating.

The first gentleman said, "May God save you, sir! Where have you been broiling?"

"Among the crowd in Westminster Abbey, where not even one more finger could be wedged in because it was so crowded," the third gentleman said. "I am stifled with the complete rankness of their joy."

The word "rankness" meant both "excess" and "bad odor."

The second gentleman asked him, "Did you see the coronation ceremony?"

"Yes, I did."

"How was it?" the first gentleman asked.

"Well worth the seeing."

"Good sir, describe it to us," the second gentleman said.

"I will as well as I am able to," the third gentleman said. "The rich stream of lords and ladies, having brought the Queen to a prepared place in the choir, withdrew a distance away from her while her grace sat down to rest awhile, some half an hour or so, in a rich chair of state, displaying freely the beauty of her person to the people.

"Believe me, sir, she is the most beautiful woman who ever lay by a man. When the people had a full view of her, such a noise arose as the mast ropes make at sea in a stiff tempest, as loud, and to as many tunes. Hats, cloaks — and doublets, I think — flew up, and if their faces had been loose, this day the people would have lost their faces.

"Such joy I never saw before. Great-bellied women who had not half a week to go before giving birth, like battering rams in the old time of war, would shake the crowd of people and make them reel before them.

"No man living could say, 'This is my wife,' there; all were woven together so strangely into one piece."

"What happened next?" the second gentleman said.

"At length her grace rose," the third gentleman said, "and with modest, moderate steps, she came to the altar, where she kneeled and saint-like cast her fair eyes toward Heaven and prayed devoutly.

"Then she rose again and bowed to the people. The Archbishop of Canterbury then laid all the royal accouterments of a Queen — namely, holy oil, Edward the Confessor's crown, the rod, and the bird of peace, and all such emblems — nobly on her.

"After that was performed, the choir, accompanied by all the choicest musicians of the kingdom, sang the '*Te Deum*.'"

The song began, "*Te deum laudamus*." This meant, "You, God, we praise."

The third gentleman continued, "So then she departed, and with the same full state walked back again to York Place, where the feast is to be held."

"Sir, you must no longer call it York Place," the first gentleman said. "That's past, for since Cardinal Wolsey fell, that title's lost. That place is now the King's, and it is now called Whitehall."

"That's true," the third gentleman said. "I knew that, but the name is so recently altered that the old name is still foremost in my mind."

The second gentleman asked, "Who are the two reverend Bishops who were on each side of the Queen?"

"They are Stokesley and Gardiner," the third gentleman said. "Gardiner is the Bishop of Winchester; he was recently promoted from being the King's secretary. Stokesley is the Bishop of London."

The second gentleman said, "The Bishop of Winchester is thought to be no great good friend to the Archbishop of Canterbury: the virtuous Cranmer."

"All the land knows that," the third gentleman said. "However, as of now there is no great breach between them. When it comes, Cranmer will find that he has a friend who will not shrink from him."

"Who may that be, I ask you?" the second gentleman said.

"Thomas Cromwell," the third gentleman said. "He is a man whom the King holds in much esteem, and truly he is a worthy friend. The King has made him Master of the Jewel House, and he is already a member of the Privy Council."

The Master of the King's Jewel House had charge of the crown jewels and other valuable items.

"He will deserve more," the second gentleman said.

"Yes, without all doubt," the third gentleman said. "Come, gentlemen, you shall go with me on my way, which is to the court, and there you shall be my guests: That is something I can arrange. As we walk there, I'll tell you more."

"You may command us, sir," the first and second gentlemen said.

In a room of the Dowager Princess' residence in Kimbolton, several people met: Catherine, the Princess Dowager; Griffith, her gentleman-usher; and Patience, her serving woman. Catherine was sick; in fact, she was dying.

Griffith asked Catherine, "How is your grace?"

She replied, "Oh, Griffith, I am sick to death! My legs, like heavily laden branches, bow to the earth, wanting to be relieved of their burden. Bring me a chair."

He did, and she sat down.

"Good," she said. "Now, I think, I feel a little relief. Didn't you tell me, Griffith, as you helped me walk here, that the great child of honor, Cardinal Wolsey, is dead?"

"Yes, madam," Griffith said, "but I thought your grace, out of the pain you were suffering, did not hear me."

"Please, good Griffith," Catherine said, "tell me how he died. If he died well, then he stepped ahead of me, perhaps to be my happy, fortunate example."

"He died well — that is how the talk goes, madam," Griffith said. "For after the brave Earl Northumberland arrested him at York, and brought him forward, as a man severely disgraced, to answer the charges against him, Cardinal Wolsey fell sick suddenly, and he grew so ill that he could not sit on his mule."

"Alas, poor man!" Catherine said. "That's a pity."

"At last, with easy stages of his journey, he came to Leicester, where he lodged in the abbey," Griffith said. "There the reverend abbot, with all the members of his religious community, honorably received him.

"Cardinal Wolsey said to the reverend abbot, 'Oh, father abbot, I am an old man, broken with the storms of state, and I have come to lay my weary bones among you. Give me a little earth for charity! Give me a grave when I die!'

"He then went to bed, where his sickness eagerly and continually pursued him, and three nights after this, about the hour of eight, which he himself had foretold should be his last hour, full of repentance, continual meditations, tears, and lamentations, he gave his honors to the world again, and he gave his blessed part — his soul — to Heaven, and he slept in peace."

"So may he rest in peace," Catherine said. "May his faults lie gently on him! Yet thus far, Griffith, give me permission to speak about and describe him — with charity, I mean."

She believed that she ought to speak with Christian charity and love about the dead, but doing so was difficult despite her good intentions.

She said, "He was a man of an unbounded stomach for power and wealth and pride, forever ranking himself as the equal of Princes. He was a man who, by underhanded dealing and incitement to evil, put all the Kingdom of England into bondage. To him, Simony — the buying and selling of ecclesiastical offices — was fair play. His own opinion was his law. In the presence of the King, he would say untruths, and he was always duplicitous both in his words and meaning. He was never seemingly compassionate except where he meant to ruin. His promises were, as he then was, mighty, but his performance was, as he is now, nothing: He promised more than he gave. In his sexual morality, he was reprehensible, and he gave the clergy a bad example."

"Noble madam," Griffith said, "men's evil deeds are recorded and live on in brass; their virtues we write in water. May it please your highness to hear me speak about his good deeds and good qualities now?"

"Yes, good Griffith," Catherine said. "I would be malicious if I did not."

"Cardinal Wolsey, although he came from humble stock, undoubtedly was fashioned to much honor. From his cradle he was a scholar, and a ripe and good one. He was exceedingly wise, fair-spoken, and persuasive. He was haughty and sour to them who were not his friends, but to those men who sought him he was as sweet as summer. And although he was never satisfied with all the wealth he accumulated, and he wanted more and more, which was a sin, yet in bestowing, madam, he was most Princely. For example, take those twin schools of learning that he raised in Ipswich and Oxford! The school of learning in Ipswich fell with him, unwilling to outlive the good man who had founded it. The school of learning in Oxford, though unfinished, is yet so famous, so excellent in scholarship, and still so rising, that Christendom shall always speak about its virtue.

"Cardinal Wolsey's overthrow and fall from power heaped happiness upon him because then, and not until then, he found and knew himself, and he found the blessedness of being little powerful. And, to add greater honors to his age than man could give him, he died fearing — revering — God."

Catherine said, "After my death I wish no other herald, no other speaker of my actions that I performed while I was alive, to keep my honor from corruption, except such an honest chronicler as you, Griffith.

"You have made me, with your scrupulous truth and moderation, honor in his ashes now Cardinal Wolsey, the man whom I most hated while he was living. May peace be with him!

"Patience, be near me still, and set me lower on this chair so that I can recline. I have not much time left alive in which to trouble you.

"Good Griffith, tell the musicians to play me that sad music I named my knell — music to announce my death — while I sit meditating on that celestial harmony I go to."

The musicians played sad, solemn music.

Griffith said, "She is asleep. Patience, good girl, let's sit down quietly, for fear we will awaken her. Gently, gentle Patience."

While asleep, Catherine had a vision.

She saw, solemnly dancing one after another, six personages, clad in white robes, wearing garlands of bay leaves on their heads and golden masks on their faces, and holding bay or palm branches in their hands.

The six personages first curtsied to her, then danced. At certain rounds of the dance, the first two personages held a spare garland over her head, at which the other four made reverent curtsies to Catherine. Then the two personages who had held the garland gave it to the next two, who danced the same rounds, and then held the garland over her head while the other personages curtsied. This done, they gave the garland to the last two personages, and all the personages did the same things that had been done before.

Catherine, as if she were inspired, made in her sleep signs of rejoicing, and she held up her hands to Heaven.

The personages danced away and vanished, carrying the spare garland with them.

The music continued to play.

Catherine woke up and said, "Spirits of peace, where are you? Have you all gone and left me here in wretchedness behind you?"

Griffith said, "Madam, we are here."

"It is not you I am calling for," Catherine said. "Did you see anyone enter the room since I fell asleep?"

"No one, madam," Griffith said.

"No?" Catherine said. "Didn't you see, just now, a blessed troop invite me to a banquet — a blessed troop of good spirits whose bright faces cast a thousand beams upon me, like the Sun? They promised me eternal happiness, and they brought me garlands, Griffith, which I feel I am not worthy yet to wear. I shall, assuredly, be worthy to wear them in Heaven."

"I am very joyful, madam, that such good dreams have come to you," Griffith said.

"Order the musicians to stop playing," Catherine said. "Their notes are harsh and heavy to me."

The musicians stopped playing.

Patience said quietly to Griffith, "Do you see how much her grace has suddenly changed? How long her face is drawn? How pale she looks? She is of an earthy coldness — a sign of death! Look at her eyes!"

According to Aristotle, four elements exist: earth, air, fire, and water. Earth is a cold, dry element.

Ecclesiastes 12-7 states, "*And dust return to the earth as it was, and the spirit return to God that gave it*" (1599 Geneva Bible).

"She is going, girl," Griffith said. "She is dying. Pray, pray for her."

"May Heaven comfort her!" Patience said.

A messenger entered the room and said to Catherine, without kneeling, "If it like your grace —"

These words were too informal for a mere messenger to use when addressing a Queen, who should be knelt to and spoken formally and respectfully to.

"You are a saucy, insolent fellow," Catherine said to the messenger.

Using the royal plural, she added, "Don't we deserve more reverence than that?"

Griffith said to the messenger, "You are to blame for using such rude behavior. You know that she will not let go of her accustomed greatness. Go on! Kneel!"

The messenger knelt and apologized, "I humbly entreat your highness' pardon. My haste made me act rudely and without manners. A gentleman, sent from the King, is waiting to see you."

"Bring the gentleman here, Griffith," Catherine ordered, "but this fellow, this messenger, I never want to see again."

Griffith and the messenger exited, and Griffith quickly returned with the gentleman, whose name was Capucius.

Catherine said to him, "If my sight has not failed me, you are the lord ambassador from the Holy Roman Emperor Charles V, who is my royal nephew, and your name is Capucius."

"Yes, madam," Capucius said. "I am he, and I am your servant."

"Oh, my lord," Catherine said, "the times and my titles now are strangely altered since first you knew me, but please tell me what you want."

"Noble lady," Capucius said, "first I want to offer my own service to your grace. Next I want to say that King Henry VIII requested that I would visit you. He grieves much for you because of your weakness, and by me he sends you his Princely commendations and greetings, and heartily entreats you to take good comfort."

"Oh, my good lord, that comfort comes too late," Catherine said. "It is like a pardon after an execution. That gentle medicine, given in time, would have cured me, but now I am past all comforts here on Earth, except prayers.

"How is his highness?"

"Madam, he is in good health," Capucius replied.

"So may he always be!" Catherine said. "And may he always flourish, while I shall dwell with worms, and my poor name has been banished from the Kingdom!

"Patience, has that letter I caused you to write been sent away yet?"

"No, madam," Patience replied.

She gave the letter to Catherine, who gave it to Capucius and said, "Sir, I most humbly ask you to deliver this letter to my lord the King."

"I will do so most willingly, madam," Capucius replied.

Catherine said, "In this letter I have entrusted to the King's goodness the model of our chaste loves, his young daughter: Mary. May the dews of Heaven fall thickly in blessings on her!

"I ask him to give her a virtuous upbringing. She is young, and she has a noble and modest nature. I hope she will deserve well. I also ask him to love her a little for the sake of her mother, who loved him, Heaven knows how dearly.

"My next poor petition to the King is that his noble grace would have some pity upon my wretched ladies-of-waiting, who for so long have followed both my fortunes — my good fortune and my bad fortune — faithfully. I dare to avow — since I am a dying person, I will not lie — that of all my ladies-of-waiting, all of them deserve on account of their virtue and true beauty of the soul and their honesty and decent behavior a very good husband. Let their husbands be noble; I am sure that those men who shall marry my ladies-of-waiting will be happy.

"My last request is for my men who serve me. They are the poorest in money, but poverty could never draw them away from me. I request from the King that they may have their wages duly paid them, and something in excess to remember me by.

"If Heaven had been pleased to give me longer life and suitable means, we would not have parted like this.

"These are the whole contents of my letter to the King.

"My good lord, by all that you love the dearest in this world, and as you wish Christian peace to departed souls, I ask you to be these poor people's friend, and urge the King to do me this last right and rite."

"By Heaven, I will," Capucius said, "or let me not be known as a man!"

"I thank you, honest lord," Catherine said. "Remember me in all humility to his highness. Say that the person who caused his long trouble is now passing out of this world. Tell him that while dying I blessed him, for so I will. My eyes grow dim. Farewell, my lord.

"Griffith, farewell.

"Patience, you must not leave me yet. I must go to bed. Call in more women to help you put me to bed. When I am dead, good girl, let me be treated with honor. Strew over me flowers that are appropriate for a maiden, so that all the world may know that I was a chaste wife all the way to my grave. Embalm me, then lay me out. Although I have been un-Queened, yet inter me like a Queen and like the daughter to a King. I can do and say no more."

CHAPTER 5

— 5.1 —

Gardiner, who was the Bishop of Winchester, was in a gallery in the palace in London. A page held a torch before him. A gallery is a long room in which the King and others could take indoor walks.

Gardiner said, "It's one o'clock, boy, isn't it?"

The page replied, "The clock has struck one."

"These should be hours for necessities, not for delights," Gardiner said. "These should be times to repair our nature with comforting repose, and not for us to waste these times."

Sir Thomas Lovell entered the room, and Gardiner said, "This is a good hour of the night, Sir Thomas! Where are you going so late?"

"Did you come from the King, my lord?" Sir Thomas Lovell asked.

"I did, Sir Thomas, and I left him as he was playing the card game primero with the Duke of Suffolk."

"I must go to him, too, before he goes to bed," Sir Thomas Lovell said. "I'll take my leave of you. Good night."

"Not yet, Sir Thomas Lovell," Gardiner said. "What's the matter? It seems you are in haste. If you can do so without causing great offence, give your friend some taste of your late business. Affairs that walk, as they say spirits do, in the middle of the night, have in them a wilder nature than the business that seeks dispatch by day. Your business must be something important."

Sir Thomas Lovell replied, "My lord, I respect you, and I would dare to entrust to your ears a secret much weightier than this one. Queen Anne's in labor, they say, and in great extremity, and it is feared she'll die in childbirth."

"The fruit she goes with I pray for heartily, hoping that it may find this a good time to be born and live, but as for the trunk of the tree, Sir Thomas, I wish it were uprooted now. I hope that the child lives and the mother dies."

"I think I could cry 'amen' and agree with you, and yet my conscience says that Queen Anne is a good creature and a sweet lady, and that she deserves our better wishes," Sir Thomas Lovell said.

"But, sir, sir, listen to me, Sir Thomas. You're a gentleman of my own way. We believe in the same form of religion. I know that you are wise and religious, and let me tell you that it will never be well, it will not, Sir Thomas Lovell, take it from me, until Cranmer and Cromwell, who are Queen Anne's two hands, aka two main supporters, and she, Queen Anne herself, sleep in their graves."

"Now, sir, you are speaking about two of the most talked-about men in the kingdom. As for Cromwell, besides being Master of the Jewel House, he has been made Master of the Rolls, and the King's secretary."

The Master of the Rolls is in charge of the records of the Court of Chancery and of documents bearing the Great Seal.

Sir Thomas Lovell continued, "Further, sir, Cromwell stands in the entrance and path of more promotions, with which the time will load him.

"Cranmer — the Archbishop of Canterbury — is the King's hand and tongue, and so who dares to speak even one syllable against him?"

Gardiner replied, "Yes, yes, Sir Thomas, there are those who dare to speak against him, and I myself have ventured to speak my mind about him, and indeed this day, Sir, I may say to you, I think I have incensed and angered the lords of the Privy Council by informing them that he is — for if I know he is, then they know he is — a most arch heretic, a pestilence that infects the land."

Cranmer supported Protestant ideas, and Gardiner supported Catholic ideas.

Gardiner continued, "Moved by my information, they have given this information to the King, who has so far listened to our complaint. Because of his great grace and Princely care foreseeing those deadly evils our arguments made clear lay before him, the King has commanded that Cranmer be summoned to appear tomorrow morning before the Council Board. He's a rank weed, Sir Thomas, and we must root him out.

"I have kept you from your affairs too long. Good night, Sir Thomas."

"Many good nights to you, my lord," Sir Thomas Lovell replied. "I remain your servant."

Gardiner and the page exited.

King Henry VIII and the Duke of Suffolk, whose name was Charles Brandon, entered the room.

King Henry VIII said, "Charles, I will play no more tonight. My mind's not on it; you are too hard for me to beat."

"Sir, I never have won anything from you before," the Duke of Suffolk said.

"You have won only a little, Charles, and you shall not win anything when I can keep my mind on my play," King Henry VIII said. His wife's giving birth was distracting his mind.

Seeing Sir Thomas Lovell, the King asked, "Now, Lovell, what is the news from the Queen?"

"I could not personally deliver to her the message that you commanded me to give her, but by her woman servant I sent your message. She returned the Queen's thanks with the greatest humbleness, and she desired your highness most heartily to pray for her."

"What are you saying?" King Henry VIII said. "To pray for her? Is she crying out in pain?"

"So said her woman servant, who also said that her suffering almost made each pang a death," Sir Thomas Lovell said.

"Alas, good lady!" King Henry VIII said.

"May God safely deliver her of her burden, her baby, and with little travail, to the gladdening of your highness with an heir!" the Duke of Suffolk said.

"It is the middle of the night, Charles," King Henry VIII said. "Please, go to bed and in your prayers remember the condition of my poor Queen. Leave me alone; for I must think about that which company would not be friendly to. I want to be alone right now."

"I wish your highness a quiet night," the Duke of Suffolk said, "and I will remember my good mistress in my prayers."

"Charles, good night," the King said.

Sir Anthony Denny entered the gallery.

"Well, sir, what is your news?" King Henry VIII asked.

"Sir, I have brought my lord the Archbishop, as you commanded me."

"The Archbishop of Canterbury?" the King asked.

"Yes, my good lord," Sir Anthony Denny replied.

"Good," the King said. "Where is he, Denny?"

"He is awaiting your highness' pleasure to see him."

Sir Anthony Denny exited to get Cranmer.

Sir Thomas Lovell, who wanted to eavesdrop on the conversation, thought, *This concerns that which Gardiner, the Bishop of Winchester, spoke to me about. It is fortunate that I came here tonight.*

Sir Anthony Denny returned with Cranmer.

King Henry VIII ordered, "Leave the gallery."

Sir Thomas Lovell loitered, hoping the King was referring only to Sir Anthony Denny.

King Henry VIII looked directly at Sir Thomas Lovell and said, "I gave you an order. Leave the gallery."

Sir Anthony Denny and Sir Thomas Lovell left the gallery.

The King frowned.

Cranmer thought, *I am afraid. Why is the King frowning like this? This is a terrifying expression. Not all is well.*

"How are you now, my lord?" King Henry VIII said. "You must want to know why I sent for you."

Cranmer knelt and said, "It is my duty to attend your highness' pleasure."

"Please, arise, my good and gracious Lord of Canterbury," the King said.

Cranmer stood again.

The King continued, "Come, you and I must take a walk together in the gallery. I have news to tell you. Come, come, give me your hand. Ah, my good lord, I grieve at what I will speak to you, and I am very sorry to repeat what follows.

"I have, and most unwillingly, recently heard many grievous — I do say, my lord, grievous — complaints about you. Having considered these grievances, we and our Privy Council have decided to summon you to come before us this morning.

"I know that you cannot easily clear yourself there of these accusations, so until there is a further trial in those charges that will require you to make your defense, you must gather your patience and be well contented to make your house our Tower of London. That will be your residence for a while. You are a metaphorical brother to us, and you are a member of the powerful Privy Council. It is fitting that we thus proceed like this, or else no witness would come against you. If you were to continue to be a member of the powerful Privy Council, no one would be brave enough to give any testimony against you."

Cranmer knelt again and said, "I humbly thank your highness, and I am very glad to catch this good occasion for me very thoroughly to be winnowed, in which my chaff and my wholesome grains shall fly apart, for I know that there's no one who is exposed to more calumnious and defamatory tongues than I myself, poor man, am."

"Stand up, good Archbishop of Canterbury," King Henry VIII said.

The King now used the informal pronouns "thy" and thou" that in this context were a sign of affection between friends: "Thy truth and thy integrity are rooted in us, thy friend. We know that thou are loyal and have integrity. Give me thy hand; stand up."

Cranmer stood up, and the King said to him, "Please, let's walk. Now, by my sanctity, I ask you, what manner of man are you? My lord, I expected you to petition me to take some pains to bring together yourself and your accusers so you could face them, and for me to hear your case completely and quickly without a distressing delay."

"Most dread-inspiring liege," Cranmer said, "The good I stand on is my truth and honesty: If they shall fail, I, with my enemies, will triumph over my personal self, which I regard as being worth nothing, if I lack those virtues of truth and honesty. I fear nothing that can be said against me."

Touched by Cranmer's innocence, King Henry VIII said, "Don't you know how you stand in the world, with the whole world? Your enemies are many, and not small in rank or in power. Their schemes and plots must bear the same proportion — they will not be small. And not always do the justice and the truth of the question carry the due of the verdict with them. A just and true person can unjustly and falsely be found guilty.

"How easily might corrupt minds procure knaves as corrupt as they to swear falsely and commit perjury against you? Such things have been done. Your enemies are powerful, and their malice is of as great size as their power.

"Do you think you will have better luck, I mean when it comes to perjured testimony, than your Master, Jesus, whose minister you are, while He lived here upon this evil, wicked Earth?

"Come on! Don't be naïve! With no good reason, you are walking along a precipice and putting yourself in danger of falling to your own destruction."

Cranmer replied, "May God and your majesty protect my innocence, or I will fall into the trap that is laid for me!"

"Be of good cheer," King Henry VIII said. "Your enemies shall no more prevail than we will allow them to.

"Be of good comfort, and this morning see that you appear before them. If they should happen, in charging you with these matters, to commit you to the Tower of London, do not fail to make the best and most persuasive arguments to the contrary, and be sure to make them with what vehemence is necessary for the occasion.

"If your entreaties will render you no remedy, and your enemies insist that you go to the Tower of London, give them this ring that they will know is mine, and there make your appeal to us before them. Let them know that you want me to be your judge."

The King handed him a ring and said, "Look, the good man — Cranmer — weeps! He's honest, on my honor. God's blessed mother! I swear he is true- and loyal-hearted, and no soul is better in my Kingdom.

"Leave now, and do as I told you to do."

Cranmer exited.

King Henry VIII said, "He has strangled his language in his tears. He cannot speak because of his tears."

The Old Lady entered the gallery.

A man yelled at her, "Come back. What are you doing?"

The Old Lady said, "I'll not come back; the news that I bring will make my boldness good manners."

She said to the King, "Now, may good angels fly over thy royal head, and shade thy person under their blessed wings!"

King Henry VIII said, "Now, by thy looks, I guess thy message. Has the Queen delivered her baby? Say, yes; and say that the Queen has given birth to a boy: a male heir who will become King after me."

The Old Lady said, "Yes, yes, my liege. And it's a lovely boy. May the God of Heaven both now and forever bless her! It is a girl, and a girl is a promise of boys hereafter.

"Sir, your Queen wants you to come and visit her, and to be acquainted with this stranger who is as like you as a cherry is to a cherry."

"Lovell!" King Henry VIII shouted.

Sir Thomas Lovell entered the room and said, "Sir?"

"Give her a hundred marks," the King said. "I'll go to the Queen."

The King exited.

A mark is a unit of money, and a hundred marks is a generous amount, but the Old Lady wanted more. If the Queen had delivered a boy, the Old Lady knew that she would have gotten more. The better the news, the better the tip, and the King wanted a male heir.

The Old Lady said, "A hundred marks! By this light, I swear I'll have more. An ordinary servant can receive such payment. I will have more, or I will scold it out of him. Did I say for this that the girl resembled him? I will have more, or else I will unsay it and say that the daughter does not resemble her presumed father, and now, while it is hot, I'll put it to the issue."

Presumably, she said this for Sir Thomas Lovell's hearing, hoping that he would give her a bigger tip.

The daughter of King Henry VIII and Queen Anne would be named Elizabeth, and she would become the great Queen Elizabeth I.

— 5.2 —

Before the Council Chamber in which the Privy Council were about to meet, a number of pursuivants and pages and footboys and so on were standing. Pursuivants are junior officers of the state.

Cranmer entered the Council Chamber and said, "I hope I am not too late, and yet the gentleman who was sent to me from the council asked me to make great haste."

He tried to open the door and said, "All locked and bolted? What is the meaning of this? Ho! Who is the doorkeeper here?"

The doorkeeper walked over to Cranmer, who said, "Surely, you know who I am."

"Yes, my lord," the doorkeeper said, "but still I cannot help you."

"Why?" Cranmer asked.

Doctor Butts entered the room and observed what was happening.

The doorkeeper said, "Your grace must wait until you are called for."

"I see," Cranmer said.

Doctor Butts thought, *This is done out of malice. I am glad I came this way so providentially. I shall immediately inform the King what is happening here.*

He exited to find the King.

Cranmer saw him leaving and thought, *It is Doctor Butts, the King's physician. As he passed along, how earnestly he looked at me! I pray to Heaven that he doesn't spread gossip about my disgrace! For certainly some who hate me have done this on purpose to quench my honor — may God change their hearts! I never sought their malice. They would be ashamed otherwise to make me wait at the door, a fellow-counselor on the Privy Council, a person of high rank who is forced to wait here among boys, servants, and lackeys. But their pleasures must be fulfilled, and I will wait patiently.*

King Henry VIII and Doctor Butts looked out of a high window, unnoticed by Cranmer.

Doctor Butts said, "I'll show your grace the strangest sight —"

"What's that, Butts?" King Henry VIII asked.

"— the strangest sight I think your highness has seen in many days."

"Where is it?" King Henry VIII asked.

"There it is, my lord," Doctor Butts said, adding sarcastically, "See the high promotion of his grace the Archbishop of Canterbury, who holds his state at door, amongst pursuivants, pages, and footboys."

Cranmer was waiting with dignity among people of much lower social status at the door.

"It is he, indeed," King Henry VIII said. "Is this the honor the members of the Privy Council do one another? It is well there's one — or One — above them yet."

The one — or One — above them was either the King or God or both.

King Henry VIII said, "I had thought they had shared so much honesty among them — at least, so much good manners — as not thus to plague a man of his high office, and so near our favor, to make him dance attendance on their lordships' pleasures, and at the door, too, like a post-messenger with packets of letters. By holy Mary, Butts, there's knavery.

"Let them alone, and draw the curtain closed. We shall hear more soon."

— 5.3 —

In the Council Chamber, members of the Privy Council were about to meet. The Chancellor entered the room and placed himself at the upper end of the table on the left hand; a seat was left empty above him — Cranmer's seat.

The Duke of Suffolk, the Duke of Norfolk, the Earl of Surrey, Lord Chamberlain, and Gardiner sat themselves in order on each side. Cromwell sat at the lower end of the table; he was the secretary. The doorkeeper stood at the door.

The Chancellor said, "Announce the topic of our business, Master Secretary. For what reason are we met in council?"

Cromwell replied, "If it pleases your honors, the chief reason for our meeting in Council concerns Cranmer, his grace the Archbishop of Canterbury."

"Has he been informed about this?" Gardiner asked.

"Yes," Cromwell replied.

"Who is waiting there?" the Duke of Norfolk asked.

"Outside the door, my noble lords?" the doorkeeper asked.

"Yes," Gardiner replied.

"He is my lord the Archbishop of Canterbury," the doorkeeper said. "He has been waiting for half an hour to know what are your pleasures."

The Chancellor ordered, "Let him come in."

The doorkeeper opened the door and said to Cranmer, the Archbishop of Canterbury, "Your grace may enter now."

Cranmer entered the Council Chamber and approached the Council table.

The Chancellor said, "My good lord Archbishop of Canterbury, I'm very sorry to sit here at this present time, and behold that chair in which you normally sit stand empty, but we all are only men, and in our own natures we are frail and susceptible to our flesh. Few men are angels, and out of this human frailty and lack of wisdom, you, who best should teach us how to act, have behaved improperly yourself, and not a little, toward the King first and then toward his laws, by filling the whole realm, through your teaching and your chaplains, for so we are informed, with new opinions that are diverse and dangerous. These new opinions are heresies, and if they are not reformed, they may prove pernicious and destructive."

Gardiner said, "This reformation must be swift and rapid, too, my noble lords, for those who tame wild horses do not lead them by the hand as they go through their paces to make them gentle, but stop their mouths with hard bits, and spur them, until they obey the orders they are given.

"If we endure and suffer, out of our easiness and childish pity for one man's honor, this contagious sickness, then farewell to all medicine, and what follows then?

"Commotions, uproars, with a general corruption of the whole state, as recently our neighbors in upper Germany can dearly witness. The Peasants' War fought there in 1524-1525 is still freshly pitied in our memories."

Cranmer said, "My good lords, hitherto, in all the journey of both my life and position, I have labored, and with no little effort, so that my teaching and the strong course of my authority might safely go one way. The goal of this effort was always to do well, nor is there living — I say this with a heart free from duplicity, my lords — any man who more detests, who more stirs against, both in his private conscience and his position, destroyers of a public peace, than I do.

"I pray to Heaven that the King may never find a heart with less allegiance in it than mine! Men who make evil and crooked malice their nourishment dare to bite the best men.

"I beg your lordship that in this case in which justice must reign, my accusers, whoever they are, will stand forth and face me, and freely speak out against me."

The Duke of Suffolk said, "No, my lord, that cannot be. You are a member of the Privy Council, and as such you are a powerful man, and because of that, no man will dare to accuse you."

Gardiner said to Cranmer, "My lord, because we have business of more importance, we will be short with you. It is his highness' pleasure, and we have given our consent to it, in order to have a better trial of you, that you be taken from here and committed to the Tower of London.

"There you will be only a private man again, and you shall know the many who will then dare accuse you boldly. They are more numerous than, I fear, you are provided for."

A person imprisoned in the Tower of London lost all power and privileges; he was a private man.

Cranmer said sarcastically, "Ah, Gardiner, my good Lord Bishop of Winchester, I thank you. You are always my good friend; if you get what you want, I shall find that your lordship is both my judge and my juror. You are so merciful. I see what you want — it is my ruin.

"Love and meekness, lord, become a churchman better than ambition. Win back straying souls with moderation, and cast none away.

"I have as little doubt that I shall clear myself — no matter how much pressure you put on me to vex my patience — as you have scruples in doing daily wrongs. I could say more, but reverence for your religious position makes me modest."

Gardiner replied, "My lord, my lord, you are a sectary — a member of a heretical sect. That's the plain truth. Your painted gloss — your specious rhetoric — reveals, to men who understand you, mere words and weakness."

Cromwell said, "My Lord of Winchester, you are a little, I beg your pardon, too sharp. Men who are as noble as Cranmer, however faulty, should still get respect for what they have been. It is a cruelty to oppress a falling man."

Gardiner said sarcastically, "Good Master Secretary, I beg your honor's mercy, you may with the least justification of anyone sitting at this table say so."

"Why, my lord?" Cromwell asked.

"Don't I know that you favor this new sect? You are not sound."

The word "sound" meant 1) theologically correct and 2) loyal.

"Not sound?" Cromwell asked.

"Not sound, I say," Gardiner replied.

"I wish that you were half as honest as I am!" Cromwell said. "Men's prayers then would seek you, not their fears."

"I shall remember this bold language," Gardiner said.

"Do," Cromwell said. "Remember your bold life, too."

"This is too much," the Chancellor said. "Stop this. You should be ashamed, my lords."

"I have finished," Gardiner said.

"So have I," Cromwell said.

"Now I say this to you, my lord," the Chancellor said to Cranmer, "It stands agreed, I take it, by all voices of the Privy Council, that immediately you shall be taken to the Tower of London as a prisoner, there to remain until the King's further pleasure is known to us. Are you all agreed, lords?"

"We are," all the members of the Privy Chamber said.

"Is there no other course of action — one that involves mercy?" Cranmer asked. "Must I necessarily go to the Tower of London, my lords?"

"What else would you expect?" Gardiner said. "You are extraordinarily troublesome.

"Let some of the guards be ready there."

A guard entered the Privy Council.

"Is the guard for me?" Cranmer asked. "Must I go like a traitor away from here?"

"Take him into your custody," Gardiner ordered the guard, "and see him safely in the Tower of London."

"Wait, my good lords," Cranmer said. "I have a little yet to say."

He showed them the King's ring and said, "Look there, my lords. By virtue of that ring, I take my case out of the clutches of cruel men, and I give it to a very noble judge: the King my master."

Lord Chamberlain said, "This is the King's ring."

"It is no counterfeit," the Earl of Surrey said.

"It is the right ring, by Heaven," the Duke of Suffolk said. "I told you all, when you first put this dangerous stone a-rolling, it would fall upon ourselves."

Proverbs 26:27 states, "*He that diggeth a pit shall fall therein, and he that rolleth a stone, it shall return unto him*" (1599 Geneva Bible).

The Duke of Norfolk said, "Do you think, my lords, the King will allow even the little finger of this man to be vexed?"

The Chancellor said, "It is now all too certain just how much Cranmer's life is valued by the King — much more than we thought! I wish that I were fully out of this mess — this mistreatment of Cranmer!"

Cromwell said, "My mind told me that in seeking tales and information against this man, whose honesty the Devil and his disciples only fight against and try to overcome, you blew the fire that burns you."

Ecclesiasticus 28:12 states, "*If thou blow the spark, it shall burn: if thou spit upon it, it shall be quenched: and both these come out of thy mouth*" (1611 King James Bible).

Cromwell continued, "Now prepare yourself for the attack that you know is coming!"

King Henry VIII had been eavesdropping outside the door. Frowning, he entered the Council Chamber and took a seat.

Gardiner said, "Revered sovereign, how much are we bound in our daily thanks to Heaven — Heaven that gave us such a Prince. You are not only good and wise, but also very religious. You are one who, in all obedience, makes the church the chief aim of his honor — you do your best to do what is best for the church — and to strengthen that holy duty, out of dear, heartfelt respect, his royal self in judgment comes to hear the case between the church and this great offender Cranmer."

"You were always good at impromptu compliments, Bishop Gardiner of Winchester," King Henry VIII said. "But know that I have not now come to hear such flattery spoken in my presence. Your impromptu compliments are too thin and bare to hide your offences. Your flattery cannot reach me. You play the role of a fawning Cocker Spaniel and think to win me to your side with the wagging of your tongue, but whatever you take me for, I'm sure that you have a cruel and bloodthirsty nature."

The King then said to Cranmer, "Good man, sit down. Now let me see the proudest man, who dares to do the most, merely wag his finger at you. By all that's holy, he would be better off dying slowly than to think even once that you do not deserve your place in the Privy Chamber."

"May it please your grace —" the Earl of Surrey began to say.

King Henry VIII interrupted, "No, sir, it does not please me. I thought that I had men of some understanding and wisdom on my Privy Council, but I find I have none. Was it discretion, lords, to let this man, this good man — few of you deserve to be called good men — this honest man, wait like a lousy, lice-infested footboy at the chamber door? This man is as great as you are!

"Why, what a shame was this! Did my warrant tell you to forget yourselves to such an extent? I gave you power to try — put on trial — him as a counselor, not as a servant. There's some of you, I see, who more out of malice than integrity, would try — vex — him to the utmost, if you had means and opportunity, which you shall never have while I live."

The Chancellor said, "Thus far, my most dread sovereign, may it like your grace to let my tongue excuse all. What was purposed concerning his imprisonment in the Tower of London, was rather, if there be faith in men, meant for his trial, and fair acquittal of any supposed crimes to the world, than malice, I'm sure, in me. For him to receive a trial in which people felt safe to accuse him, he had to be imprisoned as a private man in the Tower. Otherwise, no one would dare to accuse him and so there could be no trial."

"Well, well, my lords, respect him," King Henry VIII said. "Take Cranmer, and treat him well — he's worthy of it. I will say thus much for him: If a Prince may be indebted to a subject, I am, for his love and service, indebted to him.

"Make for me no more trouble, but everyone embrace him. Be friends, for shame, my lords!"

They did so.

King Henry VIII then said, "Cranmer, my Lord of Canterbury, I have a request that you must not deny me. That is, I have a fair young maiden — my daughter — who still lacks baptism. You must be her godfather, and answer for her."

A typical question the godparents at a Catholic infant baptism are asked is this: "Are you ready to help the parents of this child in their duty as Christian parents?" Of course, the godparents reply, "We are."

Cranmer replied modestly, "The greatest monarch now alive may glory in such an honor as to be the godparent of your child. How may I, who am only a poor and humble subject to you, deserve it?"

King Henry VIII said, "Come, come, my lord, you want to spare your spoons."

He was joking that Cramer was parsimonious and did not want to be the child's godfather because he would have to give the traditional christening gift of spoons — often one for each of the twelve apostles, each of whom was represented on a spoon handle.

He continued, "You shall have two noble partners to be godparents with you: the old Duchess of Norfolk and Lady Marquess Dorset. Will these please you?"

The infant being baptized would have two godparents of the infant's sex and one godparent of the opposite sex.

King Henry VIII then said to Gardiner, "Once more, my Lord of Winchester, I order you to embrace and love this man."

Gardiner said, "With a true heart and brotherly love, I do it."

He hugged Cranmer.

Cranmer said, "And let Heaven witness how dear I hold this confirmation."

The events that had taken place since King Henry VIII had entered the Council Chamber had shown Cranmer — the Archbishop of Canterbury — to be once again a member in good standing of the Privy Council and to have an extraordinarily good relationship with the King.

King Henry VIII said to Cranmer, using — in this context — the friendly pronouns "thy" and "thee," "Good man, those joyful tears show thy true heart. The common opinion of thee, I see, is verified. The common opinion says this: 'Do my Lord of Canterbury a malicious turn, and he is your friend forever.'"

The King then said, "Come, lords, we trifle time away. I long to have my young daughter made a Christian.

"I have made you one united group, lords, and I want you to one united group remain.

"As I grow stronger, you all the more honor gain."

Much noise and tumult were in the palace yard as people tried to get through a gate to get to a good place to see the baptism of the King's daughter or see at least the procession to and from the place of baptism.

The porter and his assistant were trying to keep the crowd back. The procession would need room to move and already the palace yard was overly crowded.

The porter said to the people trying to get inside the palace yard, "You'll stop your noise soon, you rascals. Do you take the court for Paris Garden? You rude slaves, stop your yelling."

Paris Garden was one of the noisiest places in London. It was a place where bear-baiting took place — where bears were tormented by dogs — and the animals and people made much noise.

Outside the gate, a man said, "Good master porter, I belong to the larder. That's where I work, and I need to get in."

The porter replied, "You belong to the gallows, and so be hanged, you rogue! Is this a place to roar in?"

He ordered his assistant, "Fetch me a dozen hardwood crab-apple tree staves, aka clubs, and strong ones. These we are holding in our hands are only switches — twigs — compared to them."

He then said to the people wanting to get inside the palace yard, "I'll scratch your heads with a club. You must be seeing christenings, must you? Do you look for ale and cakes here, you rude rascals?"

The porter's assistant said, "Please, sir, be patient. It is as much impossible — unless we sweep them from the door with cannons — to scatter them, as it is to make them sleep on Mayday morning, which will never happen."

Young people got up early on Mayday, a day of festivity, to go to the woods to gather branches to decorate their doorways and, no doubt, to meet the opposite sex.

The porter's assistant added, "We may as well push against St. Paul's Cathedral and try to move it away, as to try to make these people move away."

"How did they get in? Tell me, you who can be hanged and go to the Devil," the porter asked.

"Alas, I don't know," the porter's assistant asked. "How does the tide get in? As much as one sound cudgel four feet in length — you see the poor remainder —"

He lifted up his battered cudgel and showed it to the porter, and then he continued, "— could distribute, I spared no one, sir."

"You did nothing, sir," the porter said.

In his answer, the porter's assistant mentioned three men who were renowned for strength: Samson, Sir Guy of Warwick, and Colbrand.

Judges 15:16 states, "*Then Samson said, With the jaw of an ass are heaps upon heaps: with the jaw of an ass have I slain a thousand men*" (1599 Geneva Bible).

Sir Guy of Warwick killed Colbrand, a Danish giant.

"I am not Samson, nor Sir Guy, nor Colbrand, and so I could not mow them down before me as these strong men did, but if I spared any who had a head to hit, either young or old, he or she, cuckold or cuckold-maker, let me never hope to see a chine again and that I would not for a cow, God save her!"

The porter's assistant was punning. A chine is a piece of meat and 2) a fissure or a crack in skin — figuratively, a vulva. And in this culture, prostitutes were sometimes referred to as cows. Therefore, he was saying these things:

1) If I spared anyone, never let me see beef again, and that's something I would not give up even if someone offered me a cow.

2) If I spared anyone, never let me see a vulva again, and that's something I would not give up even if someone offered me a prostitute.

A man outside the gate — the one who claimed to be working in the pantry — asked, "Do you hear me, master porter?"

The porter replied, "I shall be with you presently, good master puppy."

He then said to his assistant, "Keep the door closed, sirrah."

The word "sirrah" was used to address a man of lower social status than the speaker.

"What would you have me do?" his assistant asked.

"What should you do, but knock them down by the dozens?" the porter replied. "Is this Moorfields where people gather in great numbers for military training? Or do we have some strange American Indian with the great big tool — ha! ha! —come to be exhibited at court that causes the women to besiege us so?

"Bless me, what a fry of fornication — a swarm of bastards hoping to create more bastards — is at the gate! On my Christian conscience, this one christening will beget a thousand additional christenings. Here before our gate will be father, godfather, and all together."

"The spoons will be the bigger, sir," the porter's assistant said.

Certainly the christening spoons would be bigger in number because of all the births that would occur in nine months. Also, a spoon is often used to dip into something wet, and so the porter's assistant may have meant by "spoons" penises.

The porter's assistant said, "There is a fellow somewhat near the door; by looking at his face, I think that he is a brazier."

Braziers were brass workers whose occupation required them to be around very hot furnaces.

The porter's assistant added, "On my conscience, I swear that twenty of the dog days now reign in his nose."

The dog days are the very hot days of August. They are called dog days because the Dog Star rises with the Sun in August in the northern hemisphere.

He added, "All who stand about him are under the line; they need no other penance."

"Under the line" meant "at the equator," where it is hot. Enduring such heat was a form of penance that rendered other forms of penance unnecessary.

He continued, "That fire-drake — fiery meteor — I hit three times on the head, and three times his nose discharged against me; he stands there, like a mortar-piece, aka cannon, to blow us.

"There was a haberdasher's wife of small intelligence near him who railed upon me until her pinked porringer — ornamentally pierced hat that was shaped like a soup bowl — fell off her head because she was kindling such a combustion in the state. In other words, her hat fell off because she was causing such a disturbance.

"I missed the meteor once, and hit that woman. She cried out 'Clubs!' to rally apprentices to grab clubs and come to her aid. She had seen, as I had not, in the distance some forty club-bearers who came to her aid. These club-bearers were the hope of the Strand, where she resided. They were apprentices to the merchants on the Strand, a street of fine shops.

"They battled me. I defended my place. At length they came within a broomstick's length of me. I defied them still, when suddenly a file of boys behind them, loose shot who were on nobody's side, delivered such a shower of pebbles that I was forced to draw my honor in, and let the enemy win the barricade. The Devil was among them, I think, surely."

The porter said, "These are the youths who thunder at a playhouse, and fight over half-eaten apples. No audience members, except for those who are the tribulation of Tower Hill, or those who are the limbs — think of the Devil's limbs, or helpers — of Limehouse, their dear brothers, are able to endure."

Tower Hill and Limehouse, which was pronounced with a short, not long *i* — were rough neighborhoods.

The porter continued, "I have some of them in *Limbo Patrum*."

Literally, *Limbo Patrum* means "Limbo of the Fathers." In Dante's *Inferno*, Limbo is the first circle of Hell. It is where the just people who lived before the first coming of Christ reside in the Inferno. During Christ's Harrowing of Hell, he released the Jewish patriarchs from the Inferno.

Figuratively, *Limbo Patrum* is a prison.

The porter continued, "And there they are likely to dance these three days, besides the running banquet of two beadles that is to come."

One meaning of "to dance attendance on someone" in this culture is "wait for an audience with someone." Here, it meant "wait," possibly for a judge to give the offender his punishment. The porter was playing with words, especially "dance" and "running." A running banquet was a light repast. After "dancing" at the prison, the prisoners would run through the public streets while two beadles — law officers — whipped them.

Lord Chamberlain walked over to the porter and his assistant and said, "Mercy on me, what a multitude of people are here! They are still growing in number, too; from all parts they are coming, as if we were holding a fair here!

"Where are these porters, these lazy knaves?

"You have done a 'fine' job, fellows.

"That's a 'trim, fine, excellent' rabble of people you've let in. Are all these people your faithful friends of the suburbs? Have you favored your 'fine' friends by letting them in?"

The London suburbs are the locations of the brothels.

The Lord Chancellor said sarcastically, "We shall have a great store of room, no doubt, left for the noble ladies, when they come back from the christening."

The porter said, "If it please your honor, we are only men, and what the few of us could do without being torn to pieces, we have done. Even an army cannot control this multitude of people."

The Lord Chamberlain replied, "As I live, if the King blames me for this, I'll put you all in the stocks, and quickly, and on your heads I'll clap substantial fines for neglect. You are lazy knaves, and here you are baiting bombards — harassing drunkards — when you ought to do real service and drive them away.

"Listen! The trumpets sound. They're coming already from the christening.

"Go, break among the crowd of people, and find a way for the troop of nobles to pass through fairly, or I'll find a Marshalsea — a prison — that shall keep you occupied for the next two months."

The porter cried, "Make way there for the Princess."

A man wearing clothing made of fine cloth said, "You great fellow, stand out of the way, or I'll make your head ache."

The porter said, "You in the fine clothing, get up off the rail; otherwise, I'll throw you over the barricade."

Trumpets sounded, and a procession appeared.

1. The trumpeters appeared first.

2. Then appeared two Aldermen, the Lord Mayor of London, the Garter King of Arms, Cranmer, the Duke of Norfolk with his marshal's staff, the Duke of Suffolk, and two noblemen bearing great standing-bowls for the christening-gifts.

3. Then appeared four noblemen bearing a canopy, under which was the Duchess of Norfolk, one of the godmothers, carrying the Princess, who was richly clothed in a mantle and other articles of clothing. A lady carried the train of the mantle worn by the Princess.

4. Then appeared the Marchioness Dorset, who was the other godmother, and some ladies.

The Garter King of Arms said, "Heaven, from your endless goodness, send prosperous, long, and always happy life to the high and mighty Princess of England, Elizabeth!"

Trumpets sounded, and King Henry VIII and his guards arrived.

Cranmer knelt and said, "And to your royal grace, and the good Queen, my noble partners — the other godparents — and I, thus pray: May all comfort and joy that Heaven ever laid up to make parents happy fall upon you hourly in this most gracious lady" — he was referring to the Princess Elizabeth.

"Thank you, good Lord Archbishop Cranmer of Canterbury," King Henry VIII said. "What is her name?"

Cranmer replied, "Elizabeth."

"Stand up, lord," King Henry VIII said.

Cranmer stood up as King Henry VIII kissed his daughter Elizabeth.

King Henry VIII said, "With this kiss take my blessing: May God protect you! Into God's hands I give your life."

"Amen," Cranmer said.

"Noble godparents of my daughter, you have been too prodigal in your christening gifts to her. I thank you heartily; so shall this lady, when she has learned to speak enough English."

"Let me speak, sir," Cranmer said, "for Heaven now bids me to speak, and let no one think that the words I utter are flattery, for they'll learn that my words tell the truth — this is a prophecy.

"This royal infant — may God, who is the Mover of the universe, always be near her! — although she is in her cradle, yet now promises to bring upon this land a thousand thousand blessings, which time shall bring to ripeness.

"She shall be — but few now living can behold that goodness — a pattern to all Princes living at the same time as her, and all who shall succeed her.

"The Queen of Sheba was never more covetous of wisdom and fair virtue than this pure soul shall be. All Princely graces that constitute such a mighty masterpiece as this is, with all the virtues that accompany the good, shall ever more and more be doubled on her. Truth shall nurse her, and holy and Heavenly thoughts shall always counsel her.

"She shall be loved and feared. Her own people shall bless her; her foes shall shake like a field of wind-beaten wheat and hang their heads with sorrow.

"Good grows with her: In her days every man shall eat in safety, under his own vine, what he plants, and every man shall sing the merry songs of peace to all his neighbors.

"God shall be truly known; and those around her shall learn the perfect ways of honor from her, and those around her shall claim their greatness by the perfect ways of honor, not by blood. Merit, not birth, shall determine whether a person is great.

"Nor shall this peace sleep with her after she dies, but as when the bird of wonder — the maiden phoenix — dies, her ashes will newly create another heir, as greatly admired as herself. In this way, when Heaven shall call her from this cloud of darkness that is mortal life, she shall leave her blessedness to a man who from the sacred ashes of her honor shall rise like a star and be as great in fame as she was and so stand fixed.

"Peace, plenty, love, truth, the quality of inspiring terror, all of which were the servants to this chosen infant, shall then be his, and like a vine grow to him.

"Wherever the bright Sun of Heaven shall shine, his honor and the greatness of his name shall be, and make new nations. He shall flourish, and like a mountain cedar, he shall reach out his branches to all the plains about him.

"Our children's children shall see this, and bless Heaven."

"You speak of wonders," King Henry VIII said.

Cranmer continued his prophecy: "She shall live, to the happiness of England, to be an aged Princess. Many days shall see her, and yet no day shall be without an impressive deed to crown it.

"I wish that I would know no more! But she must die, she must, the saints must have her. Yet as a virgin, a most unspotted lily, she shall pass to the ground, and all the world shall mourn her."

King Henry VIII said, "Oh, Lord Archbishop, you have made me now a man — you have now ensured my success! Never, before this happy child, did I get — or beget — anything.

"This oracle of comfort has so pleased me that when I am in Heaven I shall desire to see what this child does, and praise my Maker.

"I thank you all.

"To you, my good Lord Mayor of London, and your good brethren, I am much beholden. I have received much honor by your presence, and you shall find me thankful.

"Lead the way, lords. You must all see the Queen, and she must thank you; otherwise, she will be sick.

"On this day, let no man think he has business to work at in his house, for all shall stay here. This little one shall make it a holiday for everyone."

EPILOGUE

You readers are transported back to Jacobean England to a playhouse where *Henry VIII* has just been performed. The actor who played King Henry VIII comes out on stage and speaks this epilogue:

"It is ten to one this play can never please

"All who are here. Some have come to take their ease,

"And sleep an act or two, but those, we fear,

"We have frightened with our trumpets, so it is clear,

"They'll say it is worthless. Others have come to hear the city

"Abused extremely, and to cry 'That's witty!'

"This we have not done either. Because of this, I fear,

"All the expected good applause we are likely to hear

"For this play at this time will come in

"This play's merciful depicture of good women;

"For such a one we have showed to the good women in the audience. If they smile,

"And say that this play will do, I know that within a while

"All the best men are ours because it is bad luck and hap

"For men to withhold applause when their ladies tell them to clap."

Appendix A: Brief Historical Background

KING EDWARD I: 1272-1307

Edward Longshanks fought and defeated the Welsh chieftains, and he made his eldest son the Prince of Wales. He won victories against the Scots, and he brought the coronation stone from Scone to Westminster.

KING EDWARD II: 1307-deposed 1327

At the Battle of Bannockburn in 1314, the Scots defeated his army. His wife and her lover, Mortimer, deposed him. According to legend, he was murdered in Berkeley Castle by means of a red-hot poker thrust up his anus.

KING EDWARD III: 1327-1377

Son of King Edward II, he reigned for a long time — 50 years. Because he wanted to conquer Scotland and France, he started the Hundred Years War in 1338. King Edward III and his eldest son, Edward the Black Prince, won important victories against the French in the Battle of Crécy (1346) and the Battle of Poitiers (1356).

One of King Edward III's sons was John of Gaunt, first Duke of Lancaster.

Another of King Edward III's sons was Edmund of Langley, first Duke of York.

During his reign, the Black Death — the bubonic plague — struck in 1348-1350 and killed half of England's population.

KING RICHARD II: 1377-deposed 1399

King Richard II was the son of Edward the Black Prince. In 1381, Wat Tyler led the Peasants Revolt, which was suppressed. King Richard II sent Henry, Duke of Lancaster, into exile and seized Henry's estates, but in 1399 Henry, Duke of Lancaster, returned from exile and deposed King Richard II, thereby becoming King Henry IV. In 1400, King Richard II was murdered in Pontefract Castle, which is also known as Pomfret Castle.

HOUSE OF LANCASTER

KING HENRY IV: 1399-1413

Henry, Duke of Lancaster, was the son of John of Gaunt, who was the third son of King Edward III. He was born at Bolingbroke Castle and so was also known as Henry of Bolingbroke. Returning from exile in France to reclaim his estates, he deposed King Richard II. He spent the 13 years of his reign putting down rebellions and defending himself against those who would assassinate or depose him. The Welshman Owen Glendower and the English Percy family were among those who fought against him. King Henry IV died at the age of 45.

KING HENRY V: 1413-1422

The son of King Henry IV, King Henry V renewed the war with France. He and his army defeated the French at the Battle of Agincourt (1415) despite being heavily outnumbered. He married Catherine of Valoise, the daughter of the French King, but he died before becoming King of France. He left behind a 10-month-old son, who became King Henry VI.

KING HENRY VI: 1422-deposed 1461; briefly returned to the throne in 1470-1471

The Hundred Years War ended in 1453; the English lost all land in France except for Calais, a port city. After King Henry VI suffered an attack of mental illness in 1454, Richard, third Duke of York and the father of King Henry IV and King Richard III, was made Protector of the Realm. England suffered civil war after the House of York challenged King Henry VI's right to be King of England. In 1470, King Henry VI was briefly restored to the English throne. In 1471, he was murdered in the Tower of London. A short time previously, his son, Edward, Prince of Wales, had been killed at the Battle of Tewkesbury in 1471; this was the final battle in the Wars of the Roses. The Yorkists decisively defeated the Lancastrians.

King Henry VI founded both Eton College and King's College, Cambridge.

WARS OF THE ROSES

From 1455-1487, the Yorkists and the Lancastrians fought for power in England in the famous Wars of the Roses. The emblem of the York family was a white rose, and the emblem of the Lancaster family was a red rose. The Yorkists and the Lancastrians were descended from King Edward III.

HOUSE OF YORK

KING EDWARD IV: 1461-1483 (King Henry VI briefly returned to the throne in 1470-1471)

Son of Richard, third Duke of York, he charged his brother George, Duke of Clarence, with treason and had him murdered in 1478. After dying suddenly, he left behind two sons aged 12 and 9, and five daughters.

His surviving two brothers in Shakespeare's play *Richard III* are these: 1) George, Duke of Clarence. Clarence is the second-oldest brother; and 2) Richard, Duke of Gloucester, and afterwards King Richard III. Gloucester is the youngest surviving brother.

William Caxton established the first printing press in Westminster during King Edward IV's reign.

KING EDWARD V: 1483-1483

The eldest son of King Edward IV, he reigned for only two months, the shortest-lived monarch in English history. He was 13 years old. He and his younger brother, Richard, were murdered in the Tower of London. According to Shakespeare's play, their uncle, Richard, Duke of Gloucester, who became King Richard III, was responsible for their murders.

KING RICHARD III: 1483-1485

Brother of King Edward IV, Richard, the Duke of Gloucester, declared the two Princes in the Tower of London — King Edward V and Richard, Duke of York — illegitimate and made himself King Richard III. In 1485, Henry Tudor, Earl of Richmond, a descendant of John of Gaunt, who was the father of King Henry IV, defeated King Richard III at the Battle of Bosworth Field in Leicestershire. King Richard III died in that battle.

King Richard III's father was Richard Plantagenet, Duke of York. His mother was Cecily Neville, Duchess of York.

King Richard III's death in the Battle of Bosworth Field is regarded as marking the end of the Middle Ages in England.

A NOTE ON THE PLANTAGENETS

The first Plantagenet King was King Henry II (1154-1189). From 1154 until 1485, when King Richard III died, all English Kings were Plantagenets. Both the Lancaster family and the York family were Plantagenets.

Geoffrey Plantagenet, Count of Anjou, was the founder of the House of Plantagenet. Geoffrey's son, Henry Curtmantle, became King Henry II of England, thereby founding the Plantagenet dynasty. Geoffrey wore a sprig of broom, a flowering shrub, as a badge; the Latin name for broom is *planta genista*, and from it the name "Plantagenet" arose.

The Plantagenet dynasty can be divided into three parts:

1154-1216: The Angevins. The Angevin Kings were Henry II, Richard I (Richard the Lionheart), and John 1.

1216-1399: The Plantagenets. These Kings ranged from King Henry III to King Richard II.

1399-1485: The Houses of Lancaster and of York. These Kings ranged from King Henry IV to King Richard III.

BEGINNING OF THE TUDOR DYNASTY

KING HENRY VII: 1485-1509

When King Richard III fell at the Battle of Bosworth, Henry Tudor, Earl of Richmond, became King Henry VII. A Lancastrian, he married Elizabeth of York — young Elizabeth of York in *Richard III* — and united the two warring houses, York and Lancaster, thus ending the Wars of the Roses. One of his grandfathers was Sir Owen Tudor, who married Catherine of Valoise, widow of King Henry V.

KING HENRY VIII: 1509-1547

King Henry VIII had six wives. These are their fates: "Divorced, Beheaded, Died, Divorced, Beheaded, Survived." He divorced his first wife, Catherine of Aragon, so that he could marry Anne Boleyn. Because of this, England divorced itself from the Catholic Church, and King Henry VIII became the head of the Church of England. King Henry VIII had one son and two daughters, all of whom became rulers of England: Edward, daughter of Jane Seymour; Mary, daughter of Catherine of Aragon; and Elizabeth, daughter of Anne Boleyn.

KING EDWARD VI: 1547-1553

The son of Henry VIII and Jane Seymour, King Edward VI succeeded his father at the age of nine; a Council of Regency with his uncle, Duke of Somerset, styled Protector, ruled the government.

During King Edward VI's reign, Archbishop Thomas Cranmer wrote the 1549 Book of Common Prayer.

When King Edward VI died, Lady Jane Grey was proclaimed Queen, but she ruled for only nine days before being executed in 1554, aged 17. Mary, daughter of Catherine of Aragon, became Queen. She was Catholic, thus the attempt to make Lady Jane Grey, a Protestant, Queen.

QUEEN MARY I (BLOODY MARY) 1553-1558

Queen Mary I attempted to make England a Catholic nation again. Some Protestant bishops, including Archbishop Thomas Cranmer, were burnt at the stake, and other violence broke out, resulting in her being known as Bloody Mary.

QUEEN ELIZABETH I: 1558-1603

The daughter of King Henry VIII and Anne Boleyn, Queen Elizabeth I was a popular Queen. In 1588, the English navy decisively defeated the Spanish Armada. England had many notable playwrights and poets, including William Shakespeare and Ben Jonson, during her reign. She never married and had no children.

KING JAMES I OF ENGLAND: A MEMBER OF THE HOUSE OF STUART

KING JAMES I OF ENGLAND AND VI OF SCOTLAND: 1603-1625

King James I of England was the son of Mary, Queen of Scots, and Lord Darnley. In 1605 Guy Fawkes and his Catholic co-conspirators were captured before they could blow up the Houses of Parliament; this was known as the Gunpowder Plot.

In 1611, during King James I's reign, the Authorized Version of the Bible (the King James Version) was completed.

Also during King James I's reign, in 1620 the Pilgrims sailed for America in their ship *The Mayflower*.

A NOTE ON SHAKESPEARE

William Shakespeare lived under two monarchs: Queen Elizabeth I and King James I.

Appendix B: About the Author

It was a dark and stormy night. Suddenly a cry rang out, and on a hot summer night in 1954, Josephine, wife of Carl Bruce, gave birth to a boy — me. Unfortunately, this young married couple allowed Reuben Saturday, Josephine's brother, to name their first-born. Reuben, aka "The Joker," decided that Bruce was a nice name, so he decided to name me Bruce Bruce. I have gone by my middle name — David — ever since.

Being named Bruce David Bruce hasn't been all bad. Bank tellers remember me very quickly, so I don't often have to show an ID. It can be fun in charades, also. When I was a counselor as a teenager at Camp Echoing Hills in Warsaw, Ohio, a fellow counselor gave the signs for "sounds like" and "two words," then she pointed to a bruise on her leg twice. Bruise Bruise? Oh yeah, Bruce Bruce is the answer!

Uncle Reuben, by the way, gave me a haircut when I was in kindergarten. He cut my hair short and shaved a small bald spot on the back of my head. My mother wouldn't let me go to school until the bald spot grew out again.

Of all my brothers and sisters (six in all), I am the only transplant to Athens, Ohio. I was born in Newark, Ohio, and have lived all around Southeastern Ohio. However, I moved to Athens to go to Ohio University and have never left.

At Ohio U, I never could make up my mind whether to major in English or Philosophy, so I got a bachelor's degree with a double major in both areas, then I added a master's degree in English and a master's degree in Philosophy. Yes, I have my MAMA degree.

Currently, and for a long time to come (I eat fruits and veggies), I am spending my retirement writing books such as *Nadia Comaneci: Perfect 10*, *The Funniest People in Dance*, *Homer's* Iliad: *A Retelling in Prose*, and *William Shakespeare's* Othello: *A Retelling in Prose*.

By the way, my sister Brenda Kennedy writes romances such as *A New Beginning* and *Shattered Dreams*.

Appendix C: Some Books by David Bruce

Retellings of a Classic Work of Literature

Arden of Faversham: *A Retelling*

Ben Jonson's The Alchemist: *A Retelling*

Ben Jonson's The Arraignment, or Poetaster: *A Retelling*

Ben Jonson's Bartholomew Fair: *A Retelling*

Ben Jonson's The Case is Altered: *A Retelling*

Ben Jonson's Catiline's Conspiracy: *A Retelling*

Ben Jonson's The Devil is an Ass: *A Retelling*

Ben Jonson's Epicene: *A Retelling*

Ben Jonson's Every Man in His Humor: *A Retelling*

Ben Jonson's Every Man Out of His Humor: *A Retelling*

Ben Jonson's The Fountain of Self-Love, or Cynthia's Revels: *A Retelling*

Ben Jonson's The Magnetic Lady, or Humors Reconciled: *A Retelling*

Ben Jonson's The New Inn, or The Light Heart: *A Retelling*

Ben Jonson's Sejanus' Fall: *A Retelling*

Ben Jonson's The Staple of News: *A Retelling*

Ben Jonson's A Tale of a Tub: *A Retelling*

Ben Jonson's Volpone, or the Fox: *A Retelling*

Christopher Marlowe's Complete Plays: Retellings

Christopher Marlowe's Dido, Queen of Carthage: *A Retelling*

Christopher Marlowe's Doctor Faustus: *Retellings of the 1604 A-Text and of the 1616 B-Text*

Christopher Marlowe's Edward II: *A Retelling*

Christopher Marlowe's The Massacre at Paris: *A Retelling*

Christopher Marlowe's The Rich Jew of Malta: *A Retelling*

Christopher Marlowe's Tamburlaine, Parts 1 and 2: *Retellings*

Dante's Divine Comedy: *A Retelling in Prose*

Dante's Inferno: *A Retelling in Prose*

Dante's Purgatory: *A Retelling in Prose*

Dante's Paradise: *A Retelling in Prose*

The Famous Victories of Henry V: *A Retelling*

From the Iliad *to the* Odyssey: *A Retelling in Prose of Quintus of Smyrna's* Posthomerica

George Chapman, Ben Jonson, and John Marston's Eastward Ho! *A Retelling*

George Peele's The Arraignment of Paris: *A Retelling*

George Peele's The Battle of Alcazar: *A Retelling*

George Peele's David and Bathsheba, and the Tragedy of Absalom: *A Retelling*

George Peele's Edward I: *A Retelling*

George Peele's The Old Wives' Tale: *A Retelling*

George-a-Greene: *A Retelling*

William Shakespeare's 1 Henry IV, aka Henry IV, Part 1: *A Retelling in Prose*

William Shakespeare's 2 Henry IV, aka Henry IV, Part 2: *A Retelling in Prose*

William Shakespeare's 1 Henry VI, aka Henry VI, Part 1: *A Retelling in Prose*

William Shakespeare's 2 Henry VI, aka Henry VI, Part 2: *A Retelling in Prose*

William Shakespeare's 3 Henry VI, aka Henry VI, Part 3: *A Retelling in Prose*

William Shakespeare's All's Well that Ends Well: *A Retelling in Prose*

William Shakespeare's Antony and Cleopatra: *A Retelling in Prose*

William Shakespeare's As You Like It: *A Retelling in Prose*

William Shakespeare's The Comedy of Errors: *A Retelling in Prose*

William Shakespeare's Coriolanus: *A Retelling in Prose*

William Shakespeare's Cymbeline: *A Retelling in Prose*

William Shakespeare's Hamlet: *A Retelling in Prose*

William Shakespeare's Henry V: *A Retelling in Prose*

William Shakespeare's Henry VIII: *A Retelling in Prose*

William Shakespeare's Julius Caesar: *A Retelling in Prose*

William Shakespeare's King John: *A Retelling in Prose*

William Shakespeare's King Lear: *A Retelling in Prose*

William Shakespeare's Love's Labor's Lost: *A Retelling in Prose*

William Shakespeare's Macbeth: *A Retelling in Prose*

William Shakespeare's Measure for Measure: *A Retelling in Prose*

William Shakespeare's The Merchant of Venice: *A Retelling in Prose*

William Shakespeare's The Merry Wives of Windsor: *A Retelling in Prose*

William Shakespeare's A Midsummer Night's Dream: *A Retelling in Prose*

William Shakespeare's Much Ado About Nothing: *A Retelling in Prose*

William Shakespeare's Othello: *A Retelling in Prose*

William Shakespeare's Pericles, Prince of Tyre: *A Retelling in Prose*

William Shakespeare's Richard II: *A Retelling in Prose*

William Shakespeare's Richard III: *A Retelling in Prose*

William Shakespeare's Romeo and Juliet: *A Retelling in Prose*

William Shakespeare's The Taming of the Shrew: *A Retelling in Prose*

William Shakespeare's The Tempest: *A Retelling in Prose*

William Shakespeare's Timon of Athens: *A Retelling in Prose*

William Shakespeare's Titus Andronicus: *A Retelling in Prose*

William Shakespeare's Troilus and Cressida: *A Retelling in Prose*

William Shakespeare's Twelfth Night: *A Retelling in Prose*

William Shakespeare's The Two Gentlemen of Verona: *A Retelling in Prose*

William Shakespeare's The Two Noble Kinsmen: *A Retelling in Prose*

William Shakespeare's The Winter's Tale: *A Retelling in Prose*